THE CABIN
LUCAS PEDERSON

SEVERED PRESS

THE CABIN

Copyright © 2022 Lucas Pederson

WWW.SEVEREDPRESS.COM

ISBN: 978-1-922861-02-3

THREE DAYS EARLIER

Everything hurt. Never in his life had he hurt so much. Not even when he knocked out a couple of his teeth with a rock because of rot.

No, this hurt was different. Ever since eating the bat from the old caves north of here, he couldn't stop sneezing and his throat burned. Pain spread throughout his chest, and it felt like a bunch of bees had snuck into his head. He couldn't think much, let alone move. And he was thirsty. Always thirsty. No matter how much he drank it wasn't enough.

The pain also wasn't like what he felt when his mate died after giving birth to their son. That was a different pain. A sad pain.

He wheezed, coughed, and sat with his back against a tree. A grunt tumbled out of him, and he looked at the sky. He thought about his beloved mate. He missed her warmth and love. How she made him feel complete.

Their offspring, a male, now almost as tall as his mother, crouched nearby. The boy helped him up and led him to the stream. A series of gentle grunts and coos told him the boy wanted him to drink some water. He dropped to his knees beside the stream. Little more than a trickle. A fresh spring which they'd drunk from many times before. His entire body quaked. A raspy noise, like ripping bark, escaped his quivering mouth. He reached for the water, hand cupped and trembling, but the arm holding him up gave out and he dropped face first into the stream.

With not enough strength to lift himself out, he tried pushing with his legs to get out of the water. It didn't work and he knew he would die now. He couldn't breathe. He would die in the water and—

His son pulled him out of the stream and managed to drag him away from it some. He coughed and sputtered. A hideous shiver racked his massive frame.

In all his long life, he had never felt so close to death. Could it be he finally met his end? Too old, like his own father had been. A long time ago now, when he bashed his father's head in with a rock when father couldn't move anymore. Would his son now have to do the same to him?

No. He's not that old and the bat...something about the bat had tasted bad. Wrong. Something inside the bat...

His son helped him drink a few handfuls of water, then they ventured deeper into the woods. A storm was coming. He'd caught its scent on the air before eating the bat. The scent of snow. They would need to go deep into the caves soon and sleep for the winter like the bears do.

It hadn't always been that way. Until his mate made him do so years ago, he suffered through the harsh winters, surviving in caves and old structures and living off bark and melted snow. Maybe the occasional deer or rabbit. Sometimes a wolf. His mate found that eating a lot during the spring and summer and storing food in their deep cave, their home, and sleeping all winter was the key to a better life. Bears knew how to survive in the north and adopting their behaviors proved to work best.

Since getting sick, though, they hadn't gathered or eaten much of anything. It was going to be a hard winter. But he had his offspring, even if the boy was a bumbling creature at times. He had his son and that's what mattered.

How long ago did he eat the bat? Days? Weeks? He couldn't remember.

He stumbled and fell to his hands and knees in a patch of dying moss. His offspring crouched nearby, cooing, telling him to rest now and they would continue to the caves when he was ready. But he wasn't sure if he would ever be ready. He lay down on the cool moss and coughed so hard his throat felt like it was trying to rip itself out of him. His chest burned and it was harder to breathe than before. Shivers quaked his massive body.

The world around him blurred. The sounds of his offspring cooing and grunting faded. The sound of the forest dwindled to whispers. His sense of smell vanished. He rolled onto his side, wheezing until eventually darkness swooped in like a giant bird and took him away.

***

Paul cracked open his first beer of the day and took a quick swig.

"Took ya long enough," Josh said. He leaned forward and smacked Paul's shoulder. "Tomorrow, I wanna see ya have a beer an hour."

Paul burped and placed the beer can on the card table they all sat around. "I thought we're supposed to be hunting?"

Josh glanced at Ben and Ben looked at Chad. They were quiet for a second or two, then threw back their heads in laughter.

Paul sighed. He liked hanging out with them, they were his friends, but sometimes…

"Well hell yeah," Chad said. "We're here to hunt. Might as well enjoy the time even more, right? Away from all the bullshit. Wife. Kids. Work. Fixin' shit all the time…"

"A vacation," Ben said, raising his own beer in an awkward cheers salute. "That's what this is." He drank deeply.

Josh and Chad clicked the edges of their cans together and drank.

Paul took another drink from his beer. Another. And one more. He needed the alcohol to kick in so he could relax a bit more. They were all friends, sure, but he was the only one who had a difficult time letting loose as easily as they did. A couple of beers would cure that, though.

Always did.

This was his first time out hunting with the guys, though, so he cracked open another beer and sat back in the old wooden chair. It creaked under his weight. The rest of the cabin was just as old and creaky. Josh's grandpa had built it back in the eighties and it showed. As far as Paul knew, Josh had only done a few minor updates. Mainly to the front door and windows. Insulation too.

A small fire crackled away in the cobblestone fireplace.

It was old, sure, but it was cozy too and...

"Y'all hear that?" Ben said and stood from his own rickety wooden chair. He hurried to the only west facing window.

"Hear what?" Josh said. "Man, it's too late to go chasin'—"

"Shut up," Ben said, and the man sounded stone cold serious. Knowing his friends, though, he took it all with a grain of salt.

Hell, he almost expected a couple of strippers to burst through the door any moment.

That didn't happen. Ben drew his Smith and Wesson .41 Magnum revolver. One of the best hunting back-ups, according to Ben, anyway. The guy had talked about it almost constantly since they arrived at the cabin yesterday.

"What the hell you on about?" Chad said and stood. "Someone fuckin' around out there?" He drew his own sidearm, though this was a pistol that looked like a Colt. A 1911 in style, maybe, but without asking, Paul wasn't quite sure. He wasn't as familiar with guns as his buddies.

"Sounded like someone coughing," Ben said. "Whoever it is sounds big."

"Think Big Mel followed us out here?" Josh asked.

Ben shook his head, trying to peer through the window, though fogged it up with his breath instead. "Big Mel don't like the cold, man."

It was getting cold out there. Paul still couldn't really feel the tips of his fingers. The weather app on his phone said there was a big storm heading this way in a couple of days. Not that they would be here in a couple of days. Tomorrow was Saturday and Sunday they were going to pack up early and head home.

Chad zipped his coat up and said, "Well, I'm done fuckin' around. Whoever it is, is going to get the hell outta here or get a bullet in their ass."

Ben nodded. "Let's check it out."

"Paul and I will hold the fort down," Josh said and raised his beer. "Bag us a motherfucker."

That got them all chuckling, even Paul.

Ben and Chad opened the door and stepped out into the cold evening.

***

Voices. Strange voices. All of them pounding in his head like heavy rocks against his skull. Over and over.

He opened his eyes and groaned. He didn't hurt as bad as before and breathed better, but something was wrong with his head. Voices. Sounds. Everything was too loud. He also needed water. His tongue and throat burned. The pounding became a violent beehive in his head. He couldn't think. Nothing made sense. He stood and swayed in place for a few seconds. Something cooed, telling him to sit back down. Something else spoke to him in a language he couldn't understand. Angry rumblings. Sticks snapped under boots.

Boots…

The others. The others were in the forest. Outlings was the name he gave them. Animals that walked like he did but didn't have any fur and always spoke in angry tones. Outlings were dangerous. Was his offspring hidden? His mate? Was she…no…no she's dead. She…

Something emerged from the shadows. Something about the size of an outling. His offspring must be hidden. The boy knew what to do around the others. Bumbling creature or not. So, the thing walking closer and closer to him must be—

Never in all his long life had he let one of them get so close.

And never again.

He roared and slammed fist after heavy fist down on the outling. It wailed and dropped to the ground. He stomped on the creature until it stopped trying to get away. He stooped and clutched its head in both of his hands. It screamed as he felt its skull give. Meaty crackling filled his ears. Such a satisfying sound he couldn't help but smile.

With a final roar, he ripped the outling's head from its furless body.

His head filled with more of that beehive buzzing. He dropped the head and staggered backward into a tree. Everything went dark for a while. The only thing that mattered right then was how thirsty he was and the buzzing in his head. So loud. So constant. So…

He opened his eyes and blinked. Wasn't it getting dark before he fell asleep? If so, it wasn't now. And when was now? Two beams of light focused on something headless on the ground.

Somewhere nearby, a strange voice muttered something. Another strange voice said something else. He couldn't understand either.

All he knew at that moment was the body of his son lying not far in front of him. The dark brown fur. The slight build. Not yet gathering the bulk and height that comes with maturity. His son's head rested on its side, gaping directly at him. Mouth open. Eyes wide. His baby…his only son…terrified before…before…

He followed the beams of light to their sources standing just outside a stand of thick brush.

They killed him.

The outlings. Their stench was undeniable. Their noise…unmistakable. They did this. They killed his boy. They're the ones who scared him so bad. They tore his head off…

They…

He rose to his full height and all of his sorrow and rage spilled out in a roar.

The outlings switched their beams of light to him. One of them said something in a choked voice. Opposite the hands they held the beams of light in were other objects. These were like something he had seen before. Things of death. Weapons. Loud booms and bangs and so many dead animals. Some of those left to rot if he hadn't eaten them. He had watched it happen plenty of times while trying to hide and avoid the outlings. All he ever wanted was peace.

Until now…

He lunged, not giving them a chance to use those weapons. With all the flashing light, he didn't know what he grabbed until it was in his hands. He ripped an arm out of its socket and tossed it aside. Here…a terrified face. He twisted the screaming head off and smashed his fists into its chest. He had its heart in his hands when the other outling screamed in pain and anger.

He spun in time to see the thing pointing one of those boom weapons at him.

Not enough time to move.

Pain sliced through his left arm before the loud crack battered his ears and slammed into his head. Gone were the bees buzzing and the pounding of rocks. Now it was something worse. Something unnatural. Something beyond thought. And it beat against the insides of his skull like the tiny ice balls that fell from the summer sky during a storm. Only this was constant and much louder.

He glanced at his dead son, then loomed over the living outling. It did this. It killed his son. This creature from beyond the forests. This…monster.

A deep growl rumbled in his throat and the outling screamed.

***

"You think they're in trouble?" Paul said, zipping up his coat.

"Ben don't shoot unless he has to," Josh said and loaded six shells into his twelve-gauge pump shotgun. He stuffed a few more into his coat pockets. "Might be a bear."

9

"Won't buckshot just piss a bear off, though?" Paul said.

"These are slugs. C'mon, get your shit and let's go."

Paul made sure his own twelve-gauge pump was fully loaded and followed Josh out into the cold night.

It didn't take long to find Ben and Chad. Well, what was left of them, anyway.

"The fuck?" Josh said and shined his flashlight on something else nearby.

A carcass of some animal, from what Paul could tell. The head also appeared to be missing. The dark fur ruffled in a mild breeze. Paul backed up and glanced around, heart hammering.

"What the hell is—"

"Let's get out of here," Paul said.

Somewhere in the woods, a stick snapped.

"Bullshit," Josh said. He took a couple of pictures of the mangled bodies of Ben and Chad, and the strange headless thing. "Might be a rabid bear. Just keep an eye out." He stowed his phone and approached the headless thing.

A stick snapped. This time it sounded closer.

Paul gasped and turned to Josh. "We need to go, man. Something—"

"You're not lookin' out for that bear is what's not going on," Josh spouted. "If I get attacked, I swear to shit I'll kill you myself."

Paul released a shuddery breath and sent the beam of his flashlight in the direction of the last stick that snapped. The light shook across trees, skeletal shrubs, dead weeds—

A stick snapped somewhere behind him.

With a whine caught in his throat, Paul swung around, stabbing the darkness with the flashlight beam, heart a wild mess. The flashlight didn't catch anything unusual. No bear. Nothing. Just the same—

Another stick snapped. Again, behind him.

"Fuck," Paul said. A shiver trickled along his spine. "Something's here. We need to get back to the cabin and call for help."

"This isn't a bear," Josh said. "I…I don't know what it is. Never seen anything like it."

Paul risked a glance at his friend, swinging the flashlight with him and directly into a wall of dark fur. His breath snagged in his throat like a fishhook. All that fur, it wasn't more than a foot away. Paul could practically count the fleas.

He tried to scream or call out for Josh, but his voice failed him. Nothing more than a thin squeak escaped his mouth. All he could do was gape at that wall of fur. A deep growl trembled the icy air and Paul's bladder let go. Urine soaked the front of his pants and down the right leg.

He managed a few steps backward and brought the flashlight up.

The bright LED beam trembled on a face covered in scant fur. Amber eyes narrowed and a mouth opened to reveal large gorilla-like teeth. All the strength drained out of him. The shotgun tumbled from his hands and clattered on the ground between beast and man.

"Hey," Josh said. "What's—holy *fuck*!"

The beast, which towered over Paul a good three feet—and Paul was six-foot-three—didn't even flinch at Josh's words. Rather, it cocked its head to the side and its growl deepened. A growl that sounded a bit wheezy, Paul noted, even through the thick veil of terror. The creature sounded sick. Like it had a really bad cold. It—

Two loud cracks and the monster's eyes shot open wide. A gasp fled its toothy mouth in a cloud of white vapor.

Paul recognized the loud cracks. He knew they were gunshots. Pistol shots. Why Josh hadn't used the shotgun, though…

The beast reared and howled at the night sky. Something between pain and rage. It spun around and Paul ran. He ran with every ounce of strength he had. He ran into the cold, winter night.

And he didn't look back.

Not even when Josh began to scream.

NOW

BRETT

Blood wasn't too difficult to clean up, if you knew what you were doing.

And Brett Sullivan sure as hell knew what he was doing.

Bleach always came first. A lot of it. Depending on how much fun was had, sometimes that required over ten gallons of the stuff. And a respirator, because of the fumes. This was a quick clean method. Got the surfaces well enough. Fooled some forensic tests, though not all. The trick was to pour a few gallons of hydrogen peroxide on the area afterwards. It dissolved the blood. Once all of that is cleaned up, scrub with horseradish sauce. Rinse. Bleach. Rinse.

All in all, it wasn't that hard. You just had to be careful where all the fun happened. No wood, though. Wood absorbed blood and needed to be removed, which took up too much time and tipped forensics off.

Brett dumped the last gallon of the hydrogen peroxide onto the kitchen floor of a home he'd never stepped foot in until today. It sizzled and foamed, obliterating the blood. Using a towel, he wiped everything up and scrubbed the area with pureed horseradish and let it sit for a few minutes.

He used the same towel to clean the peroxide blood as he did to wipe up the pureed horseradish.

He waited five minutes, then poured the last gallon of bleach onto the floor.

Brett scrubbed the kitchen for about an hour and rinsed. He dried the area with a couple of towels from the bathroom, wiped down anything he might have touched without his gloves on, and called it good enough.

Before shutting the lights off and closing the back door, Brett paused. A cold breeze whispered through the open doorway and nipped at his cheeks like tiny teeth. They might find the woman next spring if it was supposed to snow as bad as the local weather people were predicting. Three feet? Yeah, unless there were a few warm days afterwards, she'd be buried for months. And that was alright.

Not bad for his final kill of the year, all things considered.

Brett closed the door and turned to the woman's backyard. She had a dog once, judging by the doghouse and chain. The motion detector light barely picked these objects out. Hand still wrapped in a handkerchief to avoid fingerprints, he unscrewed the motion detector bulb. It was around three in the morning and the closest neighbor was about a half mile away, but you could never be too careful. Even out here in the sticks.

He stepped off the stoop. The grass crackled under his boots. A cold night. Colder than last night, he figured as he walked toward the woods. Somewhere far off, an owl hooted. Brett grunted, brought out a pack of cheap cigarettes, shook one out and clamped it between his lips. He lit it the moment he entered the woods and took a deep drag. He blew smoke out in a torrent and continued walking. It would be another hour before he made it through the greenbelt to Highway 6. The woman's body was about two hours to the west, his left, shoved under a thick deadfall.

Yeah, it would take them months to find her.

Especially with all the snow coming.

Brett zipped his coat all the way up to his chin. He smoked and kept walking.

Eventually, he whistled an old tune his mom used to sing to him sometimes before bed.

He would go back home now and relax. Spend the Holidays with his son opening presents and eating too many cookies. A smile touched his lips thinking about it.

The year was over.

Time to relax until next summer.

He made his way toward town to catch a bus home.

MANDY

"Gonna be a killer," Ron Cunningham said, dropping a manila envelope on her desk. "That storm comin' in."

Mandy sighed. "Ron, you know where my mail goes."

"I do, eh? Well, Ed wanted this personally delivered directly to you."

Mandy blinked, turned away from the computer and frowned at the large envelope.

"You gettin' outta town before she hits?"

"Nope," Mandy said. "Four hunters went missing a couple days ago. Probably just some miscommunication like back in twenty-eighteen. I'll wait it out here for a couple weeks then head south for the rest of winter."

Ron grunted. "No relief?"

She stretched her back, smiled and relaxed into her chair. "Greg."

Ron blinked, snorted, shook his head, and turned toward the office door. "Good luck with that one. Make sure ya read Ed's letter." He didn't look back after leaving Mandy's office.

Mandy sighed and shook her head. Ron was a good guy but severely jaded in his older age. A bit too cynical for Mandy to tolerate for very long. He was right about Greg, though. The guy wasn't the most punctual of their little team of forest rangers. He was also lucky Ed hadn't canned his ass yet.

She picked up the manila envelope and shook it. The thing was almost as light as a feather so, knowing Ed, there was probably a single sheet of paper in there with a few words typed on it. Ed, on the cusp of retirement, refused to send emails or texts if given a choice. This day and age he didn't get much choice in the matter, and someone usually needed to help him with the email thing. In the office, however, he just had various people deliver letters from him to everyone else. It was kind of weird, but also kind of endearing.

Some people just stayed in their ways and refused to budge. They scoffed at change. Or feared it. Mandy figured the jury was out on that one.

She opened the manila envelope and, yup, it contained a single sheet of paper inside. She slipped the sheet out and tossed the envelope aside.

Amanda (Ed always called her by her birth name),

Thank you for staying through the storm to see about those missing hunters. Probably a false alarm, anyway. Better safe than sorry, though. I'm sure you're wondering why I took the time to write a letter about thanking you. A moot gesture since I have already thanked you personally.

Mandy groaned. Good God, the man could carry on forever. Maybe that's why he didn't like to text. It would take up to ten messages before he got to the damn point.

Anyway, Amanda. I will need you to wait it out for an extra week. The cabin has been well stocked, and you will have more than enough firewood to last you for a couple of months. I know you're probably wondering why and here's the reason.

She blinked. What the hell was going on here?

I fired Greg yesterday. I know. I know. I should have told you before now. I bet you're angry with me too.

Oh, she was. Everyone else was getting a nice four-day weekend due to the impending blizzard and she would be stranded for who knew how long in a goddamn cabin out in the middle of the Chippewa Forest for…what? Greg was a bit lazy, but was that any real grounds to fire the guy? He was good at everything else, and they were short staffed as it was.

No one else knows, Ed's letter continued. *But since he was your relief, I thought I should inform you, regardless. I will call Ron tomorrow and let him know he will be your relief on February 16th.*

Mandy scowled at the letter. It was only supposed to be for a week. Long enough to see if the missing hunters found their way to the cabin. After the storm, she would lead a search party. The men hadn't been missing for long. About three days. It was more than likely they were ignoring their wives' calls or their phones were off. Maybe they were just enjoying their time away from everything. Sometimes people did that. Hell, she did that. Just get away from all of it for a few days. The job. Technology. People. Everything.

The hunters would probably emerge from the forest in a couple more days wondering why everyone was freaking out.

But why was Ed making her stay until February? She returned her attention to the letter.

As you know, we don't have many rangers on the department these days. No one wants to take care of the forests anymore, I guess. Could be the world is getting ahead of itself again. I don't know. All I know is I have you, Ron, and Andy to watch that sector and need to space you all out.

Andy? But he wasn't through with all his classes yet. The kid was too green to be left alone in a cabin for months, possibly cut off from all communications. Well, unless Ed gave Andy mid-summer, which seemed likely. If so, Andy would do okay. Bears and mountain lions might be an issue but shouldn't be too bad if he kept the bear spray and a gun on him while patrolling the sector. And, if he was smart, using the Gator ATV.

I know this is a shock, Ed's letter continued. *But you three are all I have for the sector until I can hire more. I have a couple leads, but who knows. If you absolutely cannot stay until February 16th, please call me ASAP. Maybe we could work something else out.*

Thank you for all you do, Amanda. Seriously. Without you and Ron, this sector would be in ruins. I am eternally grateful.

Merry Christmas and Happy New Year,
Ed

Mandy let the letter fall from her hands. It seesawed onto the desk with a whisper. She glared at it for a long time, not exactly sure how to feel. She didn't have a partner or kids to go home to besides her dog, Bear. Which, of course, was a pet child. She would need to call Carol, her next-door neighbor and friend, to check in on her Grandma every so often. Send some money through PayPal to help with the expenses of food and entertainment.

She sighed and called Carol. Then she called Ron and Andy to make sure they were all on the same page. She didn't tell them about Greg. Let Ed fill them in later. She also made sure to direct them to Ed if they had any questions about Greg and the abrupt changes.

By the time she finished all the calls she needed to make, it was almost six o'clock in the evening.

The winter storm the weather people predicted would hit around eight o'clock. Outside her office window was nothing but gloom. A combination of winter and a gathering storm. There were still things to get yet. Ed didn't mention anything about gas for the generator, so she needed to get a couple dozen gallons just in case. Also knowing Ed, he probably stocked the place with food, just not vegetables or fruits, unless dried or canned. With the generator, Mandy could freeze fruits, though. Hell, if it got cold enough outside, she could just place containers on the back porch.

She also needed to buy some multivitamins.

Mandy left Ed's letter on the desk, packed up all the important stuff like the laptop, Wi-Fi router, and satellite phone. It had been a while since she stayed in the cabin, but she thought for sure Wi-Fi could be hooked up. She also opened the gun safe and took out the twenty-gauge pump shotgun, twelve-gauge, and a four-ten. She shoved them in the large duffle bag with ten boxes of twelve shells each. For her Smith and Wesson forty-four caliber she stuffed two boxes of fifty rounds each into her duffle bag. One hundred rounds and thirty-six shells should be more than enough for a couple of months.

She locked up the office, stowed the guns and ammo in her truck, and walked to the small grocery store, Wigley's, across the street.

Above, the sky swirled with clouds the color of gunmetal.

BRETT

He lit his last cigarette and leaned against the side of the bus shelter. Early by an hour or so, Brett had plenty of time to smoke a cigarette or two. The grocery store was on the same block, so buying a fresh pack shouldn't be too time consuming.

It was almost ten in the morning and the small town of Elder Mills was remarkably quiet. A few older folks migrated to a local café or convenience store, but other than that...the town was dead. Maybe they were all getting ready for the big storm everyone kept yammering on about, like the old man in the post office where Brett bought his bus ticket.

"Gonna be a killer," the old man had said while he stamped Brett's ticket and slid it across the counter. His glasses slipped a bit down his narrow nose. He slid them back up with a liver spotted hand and smiled. He had a remarkably thick head of white hair for someone Brett figured to be in his late seventies or early eighties. "Not to worry, though. We always say that when a big'un is comin'."

"Is that right?" Brett had said and turned to leave.

"Oh, it is. And, if I were you, I'd get a refund for that ticket and hole up here for the next couple of days. No sense in goin' out in that soup. Bus or no bus. I'm gettin' outta here at noon and makin' sure my wood pile in the garage is well stocked in case the power goes out. Sheryl, my wife, she's gone now, bless'er, used to always keep the cupboard and fridge full. I think I'll be alright, though. Say, ya might want to check in at Kerlie's Roost just up town a bit. On Main. Warren Kerlie is a good kid. Knew'im since he was a knee-high, ya know. He'll give ya a good deal on a room for a couple days and he always keeps that place well stocked with food."

Brett nodded, flashed the old clerk a smile over his shoulder, and left the post office without another word. He liked the old man. Bet there were some good stories and gossip in him for all the years he spent in Elder Mills. But Brett was trying to keep a low profile and not make too great of an impression. He needed to be a forgotten face and lost memory. Someone who didn't stick out in a person's head.

The tactic worked for almost ten years now and he didn't plan on changing it. No matter how old the clerk was. Senile or not. If the man could identify Brett's face, that was a potential threat to his discovery.

So, he left the post office and clerk without a word and he was sure the clerk had a few grumbling things to say under his breath while he sorted mail and did whatever an old mail clerk did. But, would the old man really remember the encounter days later? After a few more customers rolled through, hopefully, Brett would become a forgotten face or encounter.

Now he drew in a breath of smoke, blew it out in a steady stream before flicking the butt on the sidewalk. He thought about running across the street and buying a new pack when a woman with long, raven black hair, and wearing green pants with a green parka rushed by and stomped on the smoldering butt of his cigarette.

She shot a glare at him. "Make sure it's out before tossing it, asshole."

Brett blinked, instantly admiring her strength.

Then she hurried away. About a block or so away, she crossed the street at the crosswalk and jogged out of sight behind the town's only bank.

He stared at the corner of the bank where she disappeared.

Brett detached himself from the side of the bus stop and walked to the small convenience store across the street. There, he bought a pack of cigarettes using a twenty-dollar bill he took from his last victim and tossed his bus ticket in the trash as he left.

He found the woman dressed in green shortly after loading a few bags into the backseat of a black SUV with U.S. Forest Service and a phone number emblazoned across the back before she opened the hatch. A forest ranger. Some high school kid wheeled a cart out to the curb loaded with a few more bags and what appeared to be a couple of cardboard flats of canned goods. The rack below, from what Brett could tell, was loaded with one hundred pounds of meat wrapped in white butcher's paper.

Brett grunted, leaned against the side of the bank and lit a cigarette. The woman must be one of those super sensitive types. Maybe a prepper. And if she was a prepper, that meant she was well stocked in food, water, and ammo. It was like the holy trinity for some folks.

Or...she was just stocking up for the storm, which was going to be a "killer", ya know?

She slammed the rear hatch of the SUV, thanked the kid with a few bucks, and drove away, heading northeast.

Brett finished his cigarette and followed on foot. Vehicles were easier to identify and in such a small town, a car would be reported in no time. He pulled the hood of his parka over his head, stuffed his hands in the pockets, and walked. It wasn't cold enough to wear the parka and he was already sweating, but he didn't regret buying it a couple states west. The coat not only kept him warm, but hid his face, for the most part. Besides, everyone around here wore parkas this time of year. Just in case, you know...

About an hour of walking, he stopped and worried the woman might have turned off on one of the two crossroads he'd passed so far. Another half hour, however, he spotted the forest ranger SUV parked at a small house, which couldn't be more than a two bedroom. Maybe it was her home.

Soon enough, she packed a few more things into the SUV and headed farther north.

Brett followed on foot. Her offhanded words about his cigarette butt still bounced around inside his head like a rubber ball.

The sensation couldn't be denied. Something needed to be done about it too, otherwise it would drive him insane.

Apparently, he wasn't quite done with his time in Elder Mills…

MANDY

Memories of the man at the bus stop faded some, though it was the smoldering cigarette butt that pissed her off the most. The cause of more than a few forest fires, or close calls, in her lifetime. She didn't care who the guy was. Put the butt out completely in a designated container. It really wasn't that fucking hard. Some people liked to act like they were the only ones on the planet. Selfish bastards, the lot of them.

With all the groceries she felt she would need to survive comfortably packed into the SUV, she stopped to see her grandma before heading to the cabin. She owned the house, but Grandma took care of almost everything while Mandy worked. Including Mandy's rottweiler, Bear. A two-hundred-pound mountain of love, that dog. Not a bad bone in his body. She found him in the care of a female black bear about two years ago, which had claimed the pup as her cub somewhere along the line. The female bear also had three cubs of her own. It was extremely rare for something like that to happen, but it did happen from time to time.

She searched for possible owners of the puppy but came up empty. She even posted across the Forest Conservation social media sites and hung up a couple of puppy found flyers around Elder Mills and the surrounding towns.

Nothing.

So, she took the pup in, and he'd been her cuddle buddy for two years. The best dog a person could ever want.

"How long will you be?" Grandma asked while Mandy stuffed clothes and toiletries into a suitcase.

"Was only supposed to be for a week or two," Mandy said and struggled to zip the overstuffed suitcase. "But I guess Ed fired Greg, so I have to stay until February sixteenth." She finally got the suitcase zipped and turned to Grandma.

The woman was eighty-four, but, somehow, healthier than Mandy herself. After Mandy's parents were killed on the Fourth of July by a drunk driver when she was about ten years old, Grandma, who was Mom's mom, swooped in to care for Mandy. She owed the woman her life and passion for protecting the forests.

"I see," Grandma said and frowned. "You look a bit flushed. Alright, hun?"

Mandy smiled and lifted the overstuffed suitcase off the bed. Grandma stepped away from the doorway, allowing her to drag the suitcase into the living room.

"You have beer, right?"

Mandy snorted and glanced over her shoulder. "I'd still technically be working, Grandma."

But the woman waved a hand. "Pshh. Take the case in the fridge. I'll buy another one before the storm hits."

Mandy thought about this and the more she did the better it sounded. Yes. Beer would be good, especially on New Year's Eve.

"Okay. Get the bottle of rum from the cupboard," Mandy said and opened the front door.

"Oh, no," Grandma said in a goofy this is the end-of-the-world tone. "Not the rum!" She chuckled and disappeared into the kitchen.

Mandy loaded up the suitcase and when she returned to the house, Bear was waiting, stub-tail wagging. She laughed, crouched, and gave him a big hug. "You wanna go on vacation too, don't you buddy?"

He licked the side of her face and she hugged him tighter.

"Please tell me you're taking that damn monstrous beast with you," Grandma said and placed a full case of Coors Light and the untouched bottle of rum nearby. "He's so damn *needy*."

Mandy chuckled and stood. "I bought a couple extra bags of dog food, but it's probably best he stays here with you."

Grandma pretended to faint. "There is no God!"

Laughing, Mandy gave Grandma a hug and asked if the woman would be okay for a couple months alone with only Bear and Carol to keep her company.

Grandma waved a dismissive hand. "Oh, I'll be fine. Not my first winter. Besides…" She winked at Mandy. "There's always Big Cal next door if I ever need…assistance."

Mandy laughed and shook her head. "Big Cal is *my* age, Grandma."

"So?" Grandma waggled her eyebrows.

They both laughed, hugged each other again, and Mandy left, much to Bear's disappointment.

A little over ten miles into the forest. The missing hunters were presumed to be in the general area, though search parties hadn't turned up any evidence. There was a good chance they all lied to their families too and went elsewhere. Florida, or Hawaii. Someplace tropical. Or they merely decided to hunt in a different forest and forgot to let anyone know of the change in plans.

Anything was possible.

Still, Ed and the Sheriff figured it would be a good idea to have someone around just in case the goobers showed up.

Oh well, she would make the best of it. She had plenty of water, food and books to keep her going.

About ten minutes into the narrow dirt road leading to the cabin, Mandy made the mental note to come back in the spring to cut the ruts down a bit, even it out, and trim some branches. As it was, the SUV jostled her around while the skeletal branches of oak and maple trees screeched along the doors and tapped on the windows like eager claws. The trail would need to be widened and flattened out before it got so bad they needed to hire a contractor or two to help out.

After another ten minutes or so, she pulled up to the cabin.

It wasn't old, or new, but a refurbished thing originally built in the early nineteen-eighties. It had all the bones of the original and some of the foundation, but everything else had been updated throughout the years, including a complete structure overhaul last year. Which, in Mandy's mind, was just another rebuild but worded differently to avoid taxes.

As a result of all the updates and rebuilding, it hardly appeared weathered. The logs were still the same deep stain color and the tin roof still the same dark green. As was the shed nearby, which housed the large generator that would keep the power going so she didn't have to live entirely cut off.

Mandy put the vehicle in park, and sighed. "Well, here's to two months of solitude."

She got out of the SUV and unlocked the cabin. It wasn't very big, the cabin. Maybe about the size of her own house back in town she lived in with Grandma, minus the second floor.

The front door opened immediately to a small mudroom/foyer and sprawled into the living room where a large stone fireplace stood. Neat and all, but she wasn't sure how she felt about it being so old. Ed probably had everything inspected and repaired before her stay here, but still. She was always a bit wary around older things. Hell, she wasn't so sure she trusted her six-year-old toaster at home sometimes.

A bundle of wood rested neatly on the limestone hearth. The smell of cedar and pine filled her nostrils. Pine. That was one smell she couldn't get enough of. Sucked her right back into her childhood and camping the summers away with her Mom and grandparents at the South Pike Bay Campground a smidge south of here. A place Mandy had returned to time and again as an adult just to sit and breathe in all the lovely pine and mineral scent of the lake. All of it kissed with the char of campfire smoke.

Grandma was the only family left, though refused to return to Pike Bay without Grandpa. It was their place, she said once. It was where they would relax and forget the world for a couple of weeks, and later after they retired, a month or two. Without Grandpa, Grandma told Mandy, the love of the place is different, and she would rather remember it with him in it.

Fair enough.

Mandy unpacked the SUV and glanced around the area she would occupy for the next couple of months. The cabin rested in a large clearing surrounded by tall pine trees. The yard itself was nothing but pine needles.

Inside, the kitchen was small but updated surprisingly well and stocked full of canned and dried goods. In the refrigerator was another case of beer, orange juice, various condiments, butter, eggs, and milk. There was also a large bag of Reese's Peanut Butter Cups.

Mandy snorted and shut the fridge door. Ed knew her a little too well at times. She couldn't wait to dig into that bag of Reese's later.

For now, though…it was time to unpack and get setup for the long haul. It didn't take long. Once all the food was stored in the cupboards and fridge, she tossed her suitcase on the bed of the only bedroom in the cabin and sighed.

"Home sweet home."

She wished she had brought Bear with her. It was too quiet. Too empty…

It was almost eight o'clock at night before she finished unpacking.

BRETT

Once the front door shut and the woman was inside the cabin, Brett lit a cigarette. He sat in a thick pile of leaves and pine needles, hidden by thick, thorny brambles. Raspberry bushes? Yeah. They could be raspberry bushes. With winter just ramping up, everything was gray and skeletal in the forest this time of year. Shit, for all he knew the bushes were wild roses.

He watched the cabin through the twists and thorny snarls of the bushes and smoked. He was far enough away the woman wouldn't smell it. She might see the smoke, but given the grays and browns surrounding him, he doubted it.

A chilly breeze rustled the bushes in front of him. Tree branches clicked like grasping claws. The trees themselves groaned while they swayed. Brett was once more reminded why he didn't like the woods much. They were kind of creepy. It was almost like the trees, even the bushes, knew who he was and what he'd done. Like they could see right into his goddamn soul and freaked him the hell out every time he found himself in the woods alone. Especially in the late fall or early winter like now. No birdsong. No other sounds. Just all those trees looming over him. Judging him. Reaching out for him with those skeletal branches like ancient claws.

Brett shivered and refocused his attention on the cabin.

He would make it quick. Probably just leave her there instead of hiding her somewhere in the forest. By the look, she was planning on staying at the cabin for a while anyway. By the time anyone found her he'd be long gone. But if she had a gun there was a possibility he'd get shot and leave crucial evidence behind. With only a hunting knife, he wasn't sure how it would go down. If he owned a gun, it would make everything easier, but that wasn't how he operated.

Guns were too impersonal. Too loud.

It would have to be what it would be, he concluded.

Brett burrowed himself into a drift of dead leaves and waited for nightfall.

***

He gnawed on a bone of something he didn't remember killing while he dragged the corpse of his dead offspring behind. The taste of the bone wasn't familiar. When he closed his eyes, he saw terrified faces of outlings. Bright flashes. But that was all. Did he kill an outling? He knew one of them killed his son, but…

He…he just couldn't remember.

His throat ached for water. Violent shivers struck him every other step.

He should bury his offspring. Really should. But he couldn't. He needed to find who killed his boy, his only link to the future unless he spent months searching for a new mate in a different territory.

These thoughts were fleeting. He forgot them almost as soon as they were born. The only thought that stuck was a question. *Who killed my son*? No doubt it was an outling. But where were they hiding? The only emotions toiling within him were sorrow and hate. Pure rage. All he wanted to do was rip and tear. Crush and smash.

Kill.

All he wanted to do was kill.

Everything hurt and his thirst continued to get worse. A thirst, and like all his other thoughts and needs it surfaced and was soon forgotten. Something was wrong with him, but it didn't matter much and the worry that he might be sick also fleeted through what served as his mind at this point. Here one second. Gone the next. Repeating, though never solidifying into true revelation.

He grunted, face a rictus of pain. Upper lip curled to reveal his long canines. Ghostly plumes of vapor blew out of his mouth with every labored breath and swirled around his head before finally dissipating.

Night would be falling soon and, for a moment, he thought he smelled the wisp of smoke. A sure sign of the outlings. He stopped, eventually finding the direction of the smokey scent.

Smoke was always to be avoided, but not now.

Not after what they did…

MANDY

It didn't take long for the fire to catch and soon enough she had a nice blaze going in the fireplace. She closed the flue a bit and continued unpacking.

Getting fully unpacked and supper done was on her main priority list. The fire was a side quest of sorts. The cabin was getting a bit chilly, and she figured she'd get a fire going before it got too cold. Besides, a big snowstorm was supposed to blast this section of the world tonight and it was best to get the fire nice and hot before it happened.

Once everything was unpacked and in its place, she shrugged into her coat and beanie to go check on the generator.

There were two doors to the cabin. A front and back. Only the front had a light, so that's the door she trusted most. The bears were all hibernating or should be. Maybe there were a couple diehards or stragglers out there. Still, she liked a well-lit area wherever she was. With night falling fast the front door was the best option to avoid any surprise animal wandering close to the cabin.

Mandy made sure the Smith and Wesson forty-four pistol was still in its holster on her hip and opened the door The cold air nipped at her cheeks. She hurried to the shed and topped off the generator with gas.

When she emerged from the cabin, it was getting dark. She kept an eye out for movement or shiny eyes in the woods horseshoeing the front of the cabin, but after about ten minutes, she turned to go back inside. She stopped short of the stoop, however, catching a very faint whiff of cigarette smoke. There and gone.

Before going inside, Mandy paused in the doorway. Dusk settled over the forest. Everything was silent except for the groan of the trees as they swayed in the bitter breeze.

Her gaze fixed on a thick patch of bushes about fifty feet from the small lawn of the cabin. Raspberry? She couldn't remember what berries grew around the cabin's border, but they were specially planted as a way to help feed whoever lived in it during the summer. She frowned, because it looked like someone might be sitting in those bushes, or behind them. A silhouette slightly darker than its surroundings.

Eventually she shrugged the figure off as a stump or large drift of leaves and closed the door. She locked it and made sure all deadbolts were engaged. Top, middle and bottom. Enough to keep a couple of heavy and hungry black bears out. The cabin only had three windows. One in the living room, kitchen and bedroom. All too small for a bear or even a person to climb through. She made sure all three were locked well, along with the back door before bringing in a few bundles of wood for the night.

It was just a little after eight o'clock.

BRETT

Did she see him? He wasn't sure. At first, he thought she spotted him dead bang. But then, she went inside without a word or gunshot.

Maybe she thought he was a log, or something?

Regardless, she apparently wasn't too worried.

About fifteen minutes after she shut the door, a brisk breeze picked up, stirring the leaves around him. Unlike the other breeze this one was constant and grew stronger with each passing minute.

The killer snowstorm the town was all abuzz about was almost here. He smiled, remembering a time in his childhood with his grandparents. Christmas. He was around six years old. But Grandpa never called the storm outside a "killer", rather, it was a "bad one". Everyone in the house knew it would be bad too because Grandpa would bring in large armfuls of wood and stack it near the large woodstove in the basement of their split-level house. Grandma would protest at the mess, but only enough to get Brett and his sister giggling. His grandparents were like that. They gave each other shit often just for fun. An argument was hardly ever serious.

The snowstorm that Christmas, which was a record-setting blizzard at the time he found out later, hadn't seemed so bad. Looking through the front windows, it had a chaotic beauty about it. No one died afterwards, which was why he never took "killer storms" very seriously these days. Unless meteorologists stressed otherwise. Even then, he waited until the actual event happened.

Still, there was something different about the cold air tonight. Something telling him this storm was indeed a killer.

Brett lit a cigarette. It calmed him a bit, allowing him to think a little better.

His plan was to wait a couple hours after all the lights went off, go in, make quick work of it, wait out the storm, and walk to the next town about twenty miles northwest of here. A slightly larger berg than Elder Mills called Bemidji. He wouldn't take the woman's SUV. Too traceable. Also, another way to leave evidence.

He smoked, trying to ignore the cold, running the plan through his head over and over to make sure he got every detail right when the time came and—

Something like a howl rose above the gathering wind. Brett frowned, straightened, and glanced around. Wolves roamed the woods, he knew, but that sound wasn't much of a howl, really.

More like a strangled roar. A bear, maybe? But didn't bears hibernate during the winter?

He brushed away the dry leaves and crushed out his cigarette.

The strange howl or roar didn't happen again, but it sounded close. Too damn close. He made sure the snap holding the hunting knife in its sheath was popped open and gripped the handle while night consumed the day.

The dark felt darker now. The trees groaned louder. The dead leaves scuttled around him like conspiring whispers.

Just go in now, he thought. *Break right the fuck in. Kill her and be done with it. Safer in there than a sitting duck for predators.*

Brett barely resisted the impulse. He would love to get out of the cold and away from whatever animal was making noise out there right now.

His Grandpa once told him sound travels different in the woods, though. So...maybe the thing wasn't as close as it sounded? Or...maybe it was just the wind?

Brett shivered, shoved both hands into the pockets of his coat and flinched when the first few flakes of snow kissed his nose and cheeks. He glared at the cabin, with its small window glowing bright. It was the only thing he could really see in the dark. The smoke from the chimney. Warmth. If the woman didn't shut off the lights and go to bed soon...

MANDY

She poured herself a shot of rum and knocked it back. Both doors were thick and boasted three heavy deadlocks. One on the top, the middle, and less than a foot from the bottom. All three windows, though small, had a lock which secured them to not only the frame, but the log wall itself. She wasn't sure if the glass was really glass either.

All in all, the US Forest Service built a veritable fortress.

It worked well to keep the bears and curious humans out, she knew, regardless, all the extra stuff made her feel a bit more secure.

So secure, she didn't even bring her pistol with her to the bedroom.

It was edging past nine o'clock. The storm would be rolling in soon and no one in their right mind would be out there, let alone try to mess with her all the way out here. She made sure the recording equipment was rolling for the two cameras outside, got into her pajamas and slipped into bed. She thought briefly about her pistol. She took her holster off a couple hours before heading to bed and tossed it on the couch. The thought was there and gone in barely a blink.

Then sleep swept over her.

***

The cold white stuff wisped around him. He forgot what it was called. The smokey stench was much stronger now. He licked his lips, wishing for a stream or a pond. Anything. So thirsty.

A rabbit sprang out from some dead weeds, and he slammed a foot down, squashing it. He didn't even feel its tiny bones break. It gave only the faintest of squeals. He stepped back, bent, and picked the crushed thing up. It twitched, so small in his massive hand. A deep growl rumbling in his throat, he bit into the rabbit. Hot blood gushed into his mouth, and he sucked greedily, trying to quench his ravenous thirst.

But the rabbit was so little and his thirst too great. He sucked the thing dry, ate some of its innards and tossed the corpse away. It wasn't enough. He needed more. If water couldn't be found, blood would have to do.

His nostrils flared, drawing in the smokey stench. Yes. Where there was smoke, there were outlings. Outlings had a lot more blood than a little rabbit.

He sniffed the air, body quaking in horrible shivers, until he found a direction.

Still dragging his dead offspring, mouth and throat aching for water, blood, any kind of liquid, he made his way closer to the source of the smoke.

BRETT

He lit another cigarette. A good old Marlboro. He always bought the expensive brand after the annual three-month spree. There weren't many left in the pack now and he regretted not buying a damn carton for the road in Elder Mills. Now he would be stuck in a cabin for a while without smokes.

Brett sighed and tried to savor his cigarette the best he could.

The lights in the cabin had gone out about a half hour ago. How long did it take for REM sleep to occur? He thought it happened within an hour, but maybe it was a full hour. He couldn't remember.

While he smoked and tried to ignore the blowing snow and increasing cold, he thought about his son back at home. Owen turned eight a couple of months ago. The first birthday Brett missed since his son was born. All because of the need. The desire. The purge…

His mind shuffled through images from his memories. Owen learning how to ride a bike. How he fell over and over and over until, one day, he didn't fall. Owen, laughing and happy while he opened Christmas presents. Owen stopping what he was doing just to give Brett a hug and tell him he loved him.

Brett quickly wiped away tears and finished his cigarette, dousing it in the growing drift of snow around the thick, thorny bushes.

He hunkered down, glaring at the cabin. If not for the woman inside, he would already be halfway home by now. He pulled the parka's hood over his head as the icy winds increased. Where he sat, the snow wasn't horrible. Protected, for the most part, by all the trees and thick bushes. It was getting worse, though. Sooner or later, he would have to make his move. There just wasn't as much drive as with the others now. Yes, the woman was a bitch to him, but did she deserve to die because of it? Hell, people were, in general, assholes and he had been insulted far worse in his lifetime.

A few minutes of conflict plagued him.

He could just get up and walk away. Find shelter somewhere in or around town and ride out the next morning. His year was over, after all. Time to rest.

And yet...

This one could be his grand finale. A final send-off, ushering in a new year and plans for a different, warmer location. Maybe something tropical. Hawaii. Might make him famous since the islands weren't exactly known for murders. Even though he knew about the infamous Honolulu Strangler, the guy was too sloppy and driven by emotion.

That was the trick. Keep emotions at bay until after the kill. Release, get it done, and move on. Sometimes, being human, emotions happened, Brett knew. But he learned to keep it all at bay until the deed was done.

Yes, this would be his grand finale.

This woman asleep in their log cabin miles from civilization.

Only about another half hour more to wait. Until then…

Brett pushed the butt of his cigarette into a small drift of snow nearby and lit another.

The longer he waited, though, the worse the storm got. From nothing more than wispy flurries to an all-out blizzard in minutes. He couldn't light another cigarette even if he wanted to. The temp seemed to drop at least ten more degrees, cutting through his thick parka and sweater. He tried pulling the hood down tight and turning his back to the worst of the wind gusts, but it didn't matter which direction he turned. The wind shifted, blew back his fur-lined hood, and sliced into his face like ravenous claws.

Brett pulled the hood back up and snugged it down as best he could. Shivers racked his body.

Just another half hour, he thought. *No biggie. Just another—*

A massive gust of wind crashed through the brush and blasted his face, knocking all the air out of him. He tried to stand, fell and crawled behind a large tree. One of those groaning trees. Those watchful trees…

Eventually, the gust eased, and he was able to breathe again. Snow snaked over his right thigh in a small drift. His heart thundered. His face was wet and growing numb. Brett, hands shoved deep in the pockets of his parka, shivering, looked at the cabin. The only sign of life was a soft, reddish glow through a small window. The waning glow of a fire. A thick bed of coals to keep the cabin warm throughout the night.

Brett stood on legs that might as well be two by fours for as stiff as they were. Another wind gust about knocked him over. He looked at the cabin.

Now, with the wind increasing and the gusts fiercer, he could barely see the building through a sheet of snow.

He couldn't wait any longer. The storm would just get worse. So bad he wouldn't be able to see the cabin anymore. He'd be stuck in a blizzard and even the trees wouldn't save him. Indeed, they groaned now, as if mocking his thoughts.

Images of his son flashed through his head. Birthdays. Christmases. Learning how to ride a bike. Hundreds of happy memories all colliding in his head.

The truth of the matter was…he would die if he stayed out in this shitstorm much longer.

He only had one option…

Brett stumbled through the blistering sheets of snow to the cabin and tried the doorknob. It didn't budge. Of *course* the woman locked up. He thought about running around to try the back door, if there was one, then fumbled for the lockpick kit tucked in the inside pocket of his parka. It fell from his shivering hands into a small drift running across the stoop.

"F-Fuck," he managed through chattering teeth.

Another blast of wind shoved him into the door. Blowing snow entombed him for a few dreadful seconds before letting up. He gasped, shivering, face entirely numb now, and beat his fists on the door of the cabin.

Should've just gone home, he thought, beating on the wooden door. *Should've just—*

The door swung open and he was instantly blinded by harsh, white light.

"Who are you?" the woman said. "Give me a name."

Brett tried to rush forward but came face to muzzle with a pistol.

"Move again and I'll blow your brains out," the woman said, raising her voice above the wind. "Give me a name or I'm closing the door."

"B-Brett," he managed through numb lips. "C-Cold. Please."

He couldn't see her face because of the harsh glare in his eyes. Must be one of those high-density flashlights cops used. The woman was a forest ranger, so he supposed they got some law enforcement training. They'd almost have to.

However, his right hand curled around the handle of the hunting knife in the pocket of his coat. If she tried shutting the door, he would have to take his chances and slash his way in.

"Last name?"

"R-R-Rogers," he lied. "Please. I c-can't feel my f-f-face."

The light blinding him didn't waver. "What are you doing out here?"

"A little h-hiking. G-Got lost then the s-storm."

The glare of the flashlight shifted, and the woman stepped aside. "Get inside. Fire is over there. I'll make some coffee."

Brett hurried in and dropped to his knees in front of the fireplace. He unzipped his parka to let the heat in. The glowing coals weren't enough, though, so he shoved a chunk of wood in. It caught fire in as little as five seconds.

"Oh," the woman said and used the poker to adjust the chunk a bit. "I use that drier stuff for kindling." She picked up a large quarter of split wood from the other side of the fireplace and snugged it down into the coals. When she made sure the fire was going, she turned to Brett. "Let me take your coat and boots. I think I have a couple extra blankets you can use."

He smiled. "Thank you."

She smiled back, yet, for a moment a thin line appeared between her eyes. A small wrinkle. Did she recognize him? Maybe she did.

"I'll keep the coat," Brett said, hand still gripping the knife's handle. "If that's okay?"

Her smile faltered. "Sure. I'll go get some blankets. You can put your boots over there." She motioned to a spot near the stack of cord wood she used for the fire. A black rubber mat littered with bark. Maybe she used it to haul the wood. He didn't know.

The woman eventually disappeared into another room and Brett took off his boots. Not his socks, though. They would help mask his footprints when cops found the body. He would take his boots with him when he left, of course. Triple up on the wool socks, he wouldn't put the boots back on until he got to town where the tread would be confused with similar boot treads.

If your only outlet was murder and you had a family you loved dearly, it was always good to know how to avoid and eliminate evidence. Education was key. Experience was another. Balance of the two was key. But so was being ready for any hiccups in the plan or things not rolling out as they should.

Case in point...the winter storm driving him a little crazy and waking her up to let him in.

He adapted a new strategy, though.

Play the victim. Just a scared amateur hiker caught in a blizzard. That's all.

The woman returned with a couple of thick blankets. She draped one over his shoulders and handed him a cup of hot coffee, which smelled divine and felt like Heaven. So much so, he almost forgot why he was there in the first place.

Almost...

The woman sat on the couch, about four feet from where he was knelt on the floor. "Where are you from?"

He blinked and looked at her, coffee mug clutched in tingling hands. "Um, Iowa?"

She smiled. "You're not sure?"

Brett shook his head. "No. I mean, yes, I'm sure. From Iowa." He took a quick sip of coffee and sighed. He looked at her again. "Sorry. The storm got me all mixed up a bit. I'm a father of two and live in Iowa. Stopped here on my way through for a business trip. Thought I would get a little exercise and visit the forest my grandparents liked to camp in before heading home."

The woman kept her smile, though her eyes remained stoic. Her gaze fixed on him.

Trust was something that needed to be earned with her, he noted.

"You were just driving through," she said. "But our news stations and weather warnings would be all you heard in your vehicle."

"I listen to satellite radio," he lied. Probably the quickest lie he ever came up with. He manufactured a sigh. "Didn't know what was happening local."

"I see," she said, that thin line still present between her eyes. "Well, I'll let you warm up. There's food in the kitchen if you get hungry and the couch is yours until we dig ourselves out tomorrow."

He smiled and wasn't surprised to find it genuine. The woman was being extremely kind. More so than she had any right to be for some stranger who somehow found his way to her cabin in the middle of the woods.

"What's your name, by the way?" he asked.

She smiled back and stood. "Mandy."

Then she disappeared into a hallway just off the living room. A few seconds later, a door closed. Another few seconds came the click of a lock.

Brett sighed, sipped his coffee, and stared into the flames.

***

Hard to see. Cold. Couldn't smell the smoke anymore. The wind was too strong. So cold...

He dropped to his knees and crawled into a thicket while the winds howled and blew the cold white stuff everywhere. Shivering, he wished for his mate. He wished for his offspring. He wished for the warmth of his family.

He tried eating some of the cold white stuff, which melted to water in his mouth, but it made him too cold and didn't stop the maddening thirst anyway. He beat his large fists against the frozen ground and howled in mingled pain and sorrow.

Pain and sorrow which soon turned to rage and the thirst. An insatiable hunger to destroy and devour. The outlings...

His howling turned to a roar.

The outlings did this. They killed his mate. They fed him the bat. They killed his son. They made him hurt.

He slammed his fists over and over on the ground. Plumes of snow caught the wind and were taken away like unwanted nightmares. He roared and smashed through the thicket and back into the storm.

Kill. More emotions than real thoughts or words.

The wind settled for a short bit, revealing a smear of yellow light in the distance. His hands curled into tight fists and he sprinted towards the light.

MANDY

Sleep was out of the question tonight. Not with a strange man in her living room. The door was locked and the only way in. She had her pistol and twelve-gauge loaded and ready. Pistol on her lap, shotgun leaning against the nightstand. Just in case.

She didn't know the guy, but that didn't mean he was dangerous either. Still, her grandma taught her otherwise. Everyone was dangerous until they gave a real reason they were not. Until then…they're all out to kill you. Grandma could be paranoid, but in a case such as the one Mandy found herself in now, yeah, she didn't fully trust him.

His story seemed sound. God knew there were plenty of city people who spontaneously thought they were experienced hikers and got lost in the forest for a bit. Luckily, most of them were too apprehensive to venture too deep into the woods so were easily found.

But the man in the living room…he was over ten miles into a National Forest. He had more of a drive than the others. Either that or he was just stupid. No. Not stupid. He seemed intelligent and…aware. Even for being about half frozen to death. He appeared to be telling the truth. Yet, at the same time, something felt off about him.

Like it was all an act.

There was no Wi-Fi or data signal here, so she opened a new book she brought along for the stay.

Well, new about two years ago, anyway. There was little time to read these days so…

The wind lifted in an angry roar.

Mandy lowered her book, frowning. Something about that didn't sound—

The only window in her bedroom blew inward in a spray of what was supposed to be reinforced glass. A massive fist, followed by a furry forearm, burst through the window. The roar. It wasn't the wind, but something else.

Mandy screamed, tossed the book aside, lifted the pistol, and fired two rounds at the arm flailing through the small window. Blood splattered the wall, but the arm disappeared before she could see where she shot the creature. Frigid air filled the room. Snow whispered in through the broken window. She wasn't sure if the howl was the wind or the thing she just shot.

She jumped out of bed and grabbed the twelve-gauge.

A couple of hard knocks on the bedroom door startled a shriek out of her.

"Everything okay in there?" The man from the living room. "Heard gunshots."

She backed up, eyes still on the broken window, and reached behind her to unlock the door. "It's open."

A click and the man said, "Holy shit." A few seconds passed. "The wind didn't do that."

She wanted to scream, *no shit*, but managed to choke it down enough to hand him the pistol. "Might be a big bear." She never read anything about a bear doing something like that, breaking through reinforced glass. Didn't mean it wasn't possible, though. On the other hand, the population of bears were black bear in this region and only a grizzly or Kodiak could inflict such damage. Or a polar bear. But the likelihood of a polar bear roaming northern Minnesota was too unbelievable.

It was a fist, her mind screamed. *A fist! Not a claw! Bears have claws!*

But what else could—

"We should board that up so it doesn't get too cold in here," Brett said.

Mandy blinked, nodded, then said, "No. It could be waiting for someone to get close."

"What is it?"

She frowned at the snow wisping through the broken window. "I don't know."

"You don't—how do you *not* know? Has to be a bear, right?"

Mandy turned and stepped into the hall. "No. It's something else." She stopped and glanced over her shoulder. "Grab the black duffle bag on the floor by the bed, turn off the light, and lock the door behind you."

Brett muttered something she couldn't hear but did as he was told.

"Okay," Brett said and tossed the duffle bag on the couch. "What the hell did you see? What broke through the window?"

She was still in her sweats but strapped a holster on her hips and made sure she had an extra magazine in the pocket opposite the holster. She slid the pistol home and shook her head. "I don't know. If it was a bear, it would have to be big. Like, *really* big. An old grizzly, or Kodiak."

Brett nodded. "Okay. So, it's one of those. We should be okay in here, right? Even big bears can't break down sturdy doors like that, right?" He pointed at the front door.

"Not as sturdy as that, no. Well, maybe. Depending how big they are."

"Which is it?"

She frowned at the front door. "I don't know. Everything in this cabin was updated to keep black bears and humans out."

"But not grizzlies or Kodiaks…"

Mandy sighed. "No. Because they're not common in this region."

"Okay," Brett said after a bit. "So, call your boss, or whatever. Tell them the situation. Maybe they can send someone to—"

"There's no signal out here," she said. "I can try the satellite phone, though." She paused at the door to her bedroom. "Can you back me up? Just in case."

"Sure," Brett said and fell in line behind her.

Mandy opened the door and was assaulted by a gust of frigid air. Except for a small mound of snow under the window, the room was empty. She hurried to the closet, grabbed the satellite phone and shut the bedroom door before locking it. Brett was close. Really close. Still, he always held the barrel of the twelve-gauge toward the floor.

Maybe he could be trusted after all…

Maybe, but she wasn't stupid and wouldn't let her guard down.

Mandy slammed the satellite phone onto the coffee table and dialed Ed's home phone number. Ed was the only person she knew, except for Grandma, who had a landline. It rang for what felt like forever until a young woman's voice popped on and said, "Who are you and why are you calling on *this* phone?"

"Amanda, from the U.S. Forest Service. I need to speak to Ed—"

"He's sleeping. It's after one in the morning, you know."

Mandy blinked. It must be one of Ed's daughters. Surely not his wife.

"I know," Mandy said. "But I work for your dad, and something is—"

"Sorry, hun…wrong number."

Click.

The line went dead.

"Shit," Mandy said, instantly pissed off. She dialed the number again and got a busy signal, which meant the daughter left the phone off the hook.

Then she dialed Ed's cellphone. It went directly to voicemail, as she knew it would. Ed didn't like cellphones and wouldn't touch a smartphone with a forty-foot pole. Only reason why he even had a cellphone was for work purposes if he was away from the desk. Which wasn't too often.

Giving up on Ed, she tried Ron's phone. Only a smartphone for that one, but no answer. Of course, again, it was after one o'clock in the morning.

"Do you not have a police station nearby or something?" Brett said and Mandy almost threw the satellite phone at him.

"Yes. We have a Sheriff's office in Elder Mills, but a couple towns over, Bemidji, has a strong police force."

"So…why aren't you calling them?"

She shot a glare at him, and he actually backed away a few steps. "Because I was thinking of people who could help us sooner rather than later. Or someone who might have better information on the wildlife situation than a cop."

Brett nodded, shrugged and glanced out the living room window.

"Get away from that," Mandy said, voice close to a hiss. How could he be so stupid?

"Yeah. Right. Sorry." He moved away from the window and stoked the fire instead.

Mandy found the number for the Bemidji police and talked them into sending a helicopter in an hour or so, when the storm was supposed to weaken a bit. She gave their coordinates and hung up.

"We have a little over an hour," she said. "You eat anything?"

Brett, still poking at the fire, stopped and frowned at her. "Something just tried to break through your bedroom window and you're hungry?"

"I was talking about you. Did you eat anything while I was in the bedroom?"

"Oh," Brett said and chuckled. "No. I was just about to get another cup of coffee when I heard you scream."

She sighed. "Let's grab another cup of coffee then. I could use it anyway."

He snorted and led the way to the small kitchen where a nearly full pot of coffee waited.

Mandy took her mug down from the cupboard above the sink while Brett refilled his own cup. A minute or two later, they returned to the living room and sipped at their coffee. Neither said anything for a while. The fire crackled in the fireplace. The wind howled outside. But was it really the wind? What if it was the thing that broke through the window? What if it…

She shoved her anxiety to the wayside. She needed to stay sharp and focused. Because, if it was still indeed out there, it was strong enough to break in. Anything that could break reinforced glass like that had to be enormous and tremendously strong. They needed to be proactive, or at least come up with a plan if it really did try to break in. That was assuming the window thing wasn't just a fluke.

It had a fist, not a claw.

Not a claw…

"So, you think it's a big bear out there?" Brett said and took a drink of his coffee. "Hasn't done anything for a while. Maybe it moved on?"

Mandy nodded. "It might have gone looking for easier shelter from the storm." She sighed and leveled her gaze on him. "I'll be honest, I don't think it's a bear."

"Yeah? Then what is it?"

Her gaze drifted to the small window. "I don't know."

***

His entire arm burned.

Something inside that building hurt him. No. Not something. Some...*one*. An outling. They didn't care. All they wanted was to hurt and kill. They hated his kind. They were monsters...

The wind was so strong, it about knocked him over. The cold white stuff scratched his face like tiny, eager claws. Every time he turned his back to the onslaught, the winds would shift and claw at his face again.

He stumbled and looked back to the building where the outlings were.

They had shelter. They killed his family.

He turned to the building, gaze narrowing on a speck of yellow light through the blowing cold stuff.

His thoughts disintegrated into pure rage.

That's all that was left of him.

Rage.

BRETT

Idiot.

He let her call the cops when he should have just shot her with the twelve-gauge and figured out how to deal with whatever the fuck was trying to get into the cabin. Now the authorities would be focused on Elder Mills and the surrounding areas. Attention he didn't want and didn't need. He was a stranger in this state and, unlike the woman, could easily debunk his business trip story.

It became clear while he drank his coffee and chatted with Mandy, that he would have to kill her before the storm ended.

Which gave them about an hour.

An hour before he would have to splatter her brains all over the nearest wall. If everything went right, maybe—

Thud.

A painting of a howling wolf near the front door fell off of its nail and thumped on the floor.

"What…" Mandy said, drawing her pistol.

"Looks like our friend didn't leave after all," Brett said, heart stammering a bit. He played it off like he wasn't scared. But he was. If not a giant bear, what the hell else could be out there trying to get in?

Thud.

Another painting, this one of a deer to the right of the only window, fell.

"The walls are made of solid logs," Mandy said, though he caught a hint of doubt. "There's nothing in this area physically strong enough to break through them."

Nothing natural, anyway, he thought.

"So, the cops are on the way, right?" He moved toward the front door. "An hour?"

"Yes," she said, gaze shifting from him to the small window.

She didn't appear scared to him. Maybe a little unnerved. A bit uneasy. But not exactly scared. The woman kept her cool well under the circumstances. He supposed working a job involving wild animals and crazy people intermingling would do that to a person. Or, and this he believed more on track, she was just born with some steel in her soul. A warrior's heart, his long dead grandmother would have said.

Thud.

This time the sound came from the hall and Mandy's bedroom.

His heart quickened. He started in that direction. Stopped. "We should be okay in here, right? It can't get through the windows."

Mandy nodded, finished her coffee and poured another cup. She held the pot up and looked at him. "More? Might be a long night. If the storm stalls, it might take them longer to get to us."

Brett sighed, shrugged and let her pour him another cup, though it took him a second or two to stop the hand holding the cup from trembling. He wasn't typically afraid of anything, but whatever stalked around outside drove tiny spikes of ice into the back of his neck and clutched his guts in bony claws. Because whatever was out there couldn't be human. Whatever struck the walls of the cabin…it might very well be a real monster.

The thudding stopped, though and the only sound outside was the howling of the wind around the cabin and through the trees. The snow struck the window like someone throwing handfuls of sand at it repeatedly.

They sat, him in the recliner and her on the couch. She placed her pistol on the cushion beside her and looked at the fire. He watched her drink coffee. She seemed to space out for a bit and blinked.

He drank his coffee and looked away.

"It's not a bear," she said. "It had a fist, not a claw."

Brett opened his mouth to respond, closed it. He cleared his throat. "A…a fist?"

Mandy snorted. "Sounds fucking crazy, right?"

"Uh, yeah. Just a bit."

She sipped her coffee. "I saw what I saw. A fist. Not a claw."

"Hey, that rhymed," Brett spouted and kicked himself for being stupid.

Mandy shot him a glare. "And here I thought you might be an okay guy." Then she smiled. "It *did* rhyme, though, didn't it?"

He chuckled, kind of feeling at ease with her.

You have less than an hour to kill her, a small voice whispered in his head. *Do it quick and get out of here.*

As for the creature trying to break into the cabin…the voice apparently didn't give a shit. It was the absolute part of him. The part that gave no fucks and only wanted to scratch the itch he got every six months or so. An itch rising by the minute the more time he spent with Mandy.

On the flipside, however, he could see Mandy and him becoming good friends. They didn't know a whole lot about each other, but there was an interesting connection Brett noticed, though he'd be damned if he knew what the hell it was exactly.

He thought about the hunting knife in his coat pocket.

He thought about the shotgun resting in his lap, muzzle pointed away from Mandy.

He drank his coffee and stared into the fire.

MANDY

Brett felt a bit off, though she couldn't pin down why. He surprised her a bit with the humor. Something he hadn't shown until now. Then again…maybe he was getting more comfortable around her? Hard to tell. Despite this, there was just something…strange about him. Either that, or she was just letting her mind run wild while trying to figure out what to do.

The creature couldn't get in. That much was obvious with all the thudding. So, all they needed to do was wait, right? Just chill until the storm goes away and the police can send in a rescue copter. By then, even the creature, realizing it couldn't get inside, would move on to find easier shelter.

Why it hadn't moved on yet was beyond her.

Or maybe it had? About ten minutes had passed and no new thuds or anything. Unless the constant howling from outside was really the beast and not the wind. If so…they were in trouble. The very thought sent a series of shivers through her.

Images of a hulking beast lumbering through a blizzard, stalking a small cabin, plagued her.

And yet a tiny thing called hope told her the thing had moved on.

"Look," she said. "When they lift us off to Bemidji, you wanna grab a beer or something?"

Brett shot her a doubletake but smiled. "Sure."

A loud thump yanked her attention to the fireplace. Soot sifted from the chimney and crackled in the fire. Tiny sparks snapped in the air.

Mandy stood, pistol in hand.

Another heavy thump and the bricks behind the fire trembled. More soot fell from the chimney. One of the cords of wood rolled out onto the hearth.

Brett used the poker and guided the smoldering chunk back into the fire. He backed away. He was breathing heavy, face sheened with sweat.

"The bricks moved," he whispered. "Did you see the bricks move?"

Swallowing a hard lump in her throat, she nodded. "Yeah."

"Chimneys are strong, right?"

Mandy opened her mouth to reply when the living room window exploded inward, spraying glass at them.

"Ah, *fuck*," Brett said, dropping to a knee. One hand cupped the side of his face while the other still held onto the shotgun.

Icy air whooshed through the broken window. The fire fluttered. Snow blew in so hard it was like a constant white stream. Already a drift of snow was forming from the window to the recliner.

Mandy, pistol pointed at the window, placed a hand on Brett's shoulder. "You okay?"

"I think there's glass in my eye."

"What?"

Brett spun, nearly knocking Mandy off her feet. "Did I fucking stutter? There's glass in my eye!"

She forgave him for reacting violently. She'd probably do the same.

Mandy grabbed an arm and led him from the living room to the kitchen. She tried to move his hand so she could see, but he screamed and thrashed out too much. Blood dripped from between his fingers, splattering the white linoleum.

"I need to see," she said, gripping the arm holding his face tight. She yanked him in close. "If you want me to help you, you need to listen."

Brett flailed a bit, then moved the blood smeared hand away from the left side of his face.

Mandy, somehow, managed to contain her gasp. The entire left side of Brett's face sparkled with tiny shards of glass. The largest of the shards was embedded in the outer corner of his eye.

She plucked it out without warning.

Brett sucked a sharp breath in through his teeth and pushed her away.

"Hold still," she said, reaching out for him. "There's a lot of glass in—"

A massive thump and the backside of the fireplace bowed inward. Fiery chunks of wood and hot coals tumbled out. A few rolled onto the rug near the hearth and instantly set it ablaze.

"Shit," Mandy said, grabbing the remaining pot of coffee, and dumping it on the rug.

Brett picked up the small shovel used to remove ashes and scooped most of the coals back into the fireplace followed by the burning lengths of wood.

Mandy's gaze fixed on the bricks behind the fire. Those that were bowed inward. The mortar was broken. The bricks were loose. Another good hit and that would be that. The creature had found the cabin's weakness.

"It's going to break through," she said, still staring at the fireplace.

"What?" Brett said. "I thought it couldn't—"

"The bricks aren't solid like the logs or doors."

The creature struck the front door, as if it heard her. Maybe it did. The window was broken, after all. Maybe it understood what they were saying and was toying with them now. It explained the sudden changes. The fireplace, window, back to the fireplace...the front door.

It slammed into the front door again; this time she watched it shake on its hinges. All the air leaked from her lungs. Whatever was out there was massive enough to do damage. Mandy breathed and turned to Brett. The entire left side of his face was smeared with blood. His left eye squinted at her while the right was wide and shifted back and forth in its socket.

"I have a twelve-gauge in the bag," she said and pointed at her large duffel bag. "It will pack more of a punch than that twenty."

Brett glanced at the shotgun in his hands then the duffel bag on the couch. "You really think I'll need something bigger?"

Mandy unzipped the duffle bag and brought out the twelve-gauge. "I know you will."

BRETT

His face hurt like hell. His head throbbed. His body quaked with shivers.

Still, Brett placed the twenty-gauge on the couch and took the twelve-gauge. Mandy gave him the correct slugs and he loaded five. Not buckshot like he had with the twenty.

"We use twelve-gauges for big bears," Mandy said and brought out another shotgun he thought might be a four-ten.

"Christ," he said. "Were you expecting to go to war?"

She snorted. "When you're trapped out in the wilderness alone, it's you against whatever she throws your way. Best to be prepared for anything." She loaded the four-ten, grabbed the duffel bag, which also held some ammo, he noted, and tossed it toward the kitchen. She leaned the twenty-gauge near the refrigerator. "This one is for backup only. Just in case things go wrong."

"What do you think is gonna happen?" he asked, though he kind of knew. Her saying it would confirm it.

"It's going to break through the fireplace bricks. Once it does, we'll shoot until it stops moving. You on the left, me on the right. There's a box of slugs for your twelve. We shoot four, reload. Shoot four. Reload. Don't go empty. It might charge while we're reloading."

Brett blinked. "You...you think it will take that much to kill it?"

"I don't know," she said and moved the couch in front of the fireplace. An obstacle for whatever broke through, he assumed. "Be prepared for anything, remember?"

He nodded, glanced at the twelve-gauge in his hands then the bowed-in bricks behind the fire. Mandy, with her box of shells, moved to the right of the fireplace while he found his spot a good distance from the broken window and cold wind, and there they waited.

And waited.

Brett wasn't sure how much time passed before Mandy lowered her gun and sighed. "Looks like it wants to play games."

Somewhere outside, a roar lifted above the howling wind through the window. It lasted for a few minutes, then the storm swallowed it up.

"Sounds like it might be moving away from us," Mandy said. "Maybe it gave up. With the storm, it's probably disoriented too."

"God, I fuckin' hope so," Brett said and winced when he smiled, forgetting he still had glass in his face.

He plopped into the recliner and looked at Mandy. "Can you get this stuff out of my face?"

"I have tweezers in my bathroom bag. I think it'll leave us alone now, so we have time. Need to patch up the windows before calling it a night too."

Brett nodded, wishing she'd stop talking and just get the fucking glass out of his face already. That was the problem with most of society these days. No one ever shut up and listened or just plain shut up. The noise was a constant stream.

Mandy returned to the living room with the tweezers, and spent an ungodly amount of time plucking tiny slivers of glass out of his face. He gritted his teeth. Hissed. Wanted to punch her at least twice when a sliver was being particularly difficult. All in all, though, Mandy did great.

She pulled what she believed was the last sliver and smiled. "Instead of Pinhead, we'll call you Shardhead."

He rolled his eyes. "Great. I'm a knock-off Cenobite."

They laughed and she patched him up as best she could with antibiotic ointment and Band-Aids.

"Remember when I said to be prepared for anything?" she said while smoothing down the final Band-Aid.

"Yeah?"

She stepped back and held up a small, clear plastic medical bag. "I forgot the medical supplies."

He wasn't sure what to say so smiled a little.

Mandy sighed and tossed the bag on the nearest end table. "I'm just happy that thing decided to—"

A massive crash and the fireplace collapsed in a plume of black smoke.

Brett shot out of the recliner, stumbled over his own feet and crawled toward the kitchen. The black smoke filled the cabin, blinding and choking him all at once. He stood and frantically swept his free arm about, searching for Mandy. He forgot about the black smoke for a second, sucked in a breath to call out to her, and dropped to his knees coughing.

Then someone grabbed his shirt and led him through the noxious smoke. A pillar of light opened, and he was shoved through, again, falling to his knees. A loud slam and Mandy said, "Now our only source of heat is from the generator." A pause. "We need to board up this window."

She was spouting all of this, on and on, while he remained on his knees gasping and coughing. His eyes burned and his throat burned like he swallowed part of a pizza roll fresh out of the microwave. The burning turned to a dry ache.

"Need," he coughed. "Need water."

Mandy hunkered down in front of him. She frowned. "You must've gotten a direct blow from all the ash and smoke." She glanced away for a second or two, then looked at him. "I have bottled water in the kitchen. Just stay put."

He wanted to tell her no and he'd be okay. Don't risk going out there. The monster might be waiting. Don't—

But the door closed before he could open his mouth.

Eventually, he took in the room he knelt in. Mandy's bedroom. His sore, watery eyes lifted from the shattered glass—now partially covered in snow—on the floor to the small broken window. He watched through blurry vision as snow whispered through the jagged opening. He blinked and tears trickled down his cheeks. As his vision cleared, he noted the wisps of dark brown fur clinging to the glass still stuck in the frame.

Brett swayed a bit. Could this really be happening? He was going to kill the woman only a few hours ago and now…

And now…

There was some rampaging beast outside trying to get in and she was mending his wounds.

Sometimes reality was stranger than fiction.

He couldn't kill her now. They needed to work together to stop the monster from getting in. It was fucked up, yes, but necessary. Of course, that's ignoring the possibility it might already be in the cabin. Maybe it quietly crushed Mandy's throat with one of its huge hands. Soon the door would open, and it would have to crouch to get through the doorway. He might see it before it bashed his head in. Or maybe it would simply tear his head off and crush it under a big foot. Maybe…

The door creaked open, and a breath snagged in his throat like a fishhook. His entire body quaked in a series of shivers and his stomach churned. Brett's hands gripped the twelve-gauge shotgun.

A floorboard groaned. Otherwise, the cabin remained silent save for the howling of the storm.

Brett's heart slammed against his ribs.

It was right behind him now. *Looming.* Its mouth, a beartrap filled with long teeth, hands like claws. His finger slipped across the trigger of the shotgun.

Don't go out without a fight, he told himself. *Just turn and shoot. Don't think. Just turn and—*

"Okay," Mandy said and Brett pulled the trigger.

The slug destroyed the door of the closet and Brett, still kneeling, dropped the gun. He couldn't scream. Couldn't breathe. Nothing.

"Jesus," Mandy said and swept the shotgun away from him. "What's wrong?"

She hunkered down in front of him again, face a mural of concern. That thin line between her eyes returned too, he noticed. Vaguely. His heart beat so fast he thought it might bust out of his chest and hop away. He shook his head and, oddly enough, managed a chuckle. No humor in it, but a small way to release the stress and terror boiling over inside him.

The line between Mandy's eyes deepened. "You okay?"

It took him a minute or two to nod. "Just…just my imagination running wild." His voice was barely a croak.

Snow sifted down over them and Mandy flinched at its cold touch. "Come on. Let's get you over to the bed and wash some of the soot out of your eyes."

He stood with her help and his gaze drifted to the open door.

Beyond lay only deep, cold darkness.

And whatever hid within it…

MANDY

She didn't know what to do.

Brett was having some kind of panic attack or breakdown. The fireplace and most likely the chimney were destroyed. Cold air poured in through the broken windows. In the shed, she heard the generator chugging away when the wind would let up. How much gas was left? Two gallons? One? Almost empty?

She needed to check because without the generator they might freeze to death. Even if the cops said they would dispatch a helicopter, she knew they wouldn't budge until the winds died down and the snow settled a bit. Safety first, and all that. If the storm stalls, which was one of the predictions the weather people talked about, they would be trapped for hours, if not days.

After she washed Brett's eyes out and handed him a towel to dry off, she frowned at the broken window. The cold and snow were trying to lay claim to the room. Hell, the entire house.

Once the windows were boarded up, she would focus on the generator.

Until then…

Brett coughed after trying to drink some water and splashed vomit onto the floor.

Mandy sighed, grabbed a towel and went about cleaning up the mess. The man was definitely a city guy. He wasn't handling any of this very well. The smoke and ash or soot in the face was bad, but everything else…like killing her closet with a twelve-gauge slug for instance…she wasn't sure she could trust him to do anything. If he couldn't then he would just have to sit there. Not the first time she had to do things by herself and wouldn't be the last.

A large piece of the ruined closet door caught her eye and she gestured to it. "I have some screws and a power screwdriver in the kitchen. We can patch that hole up in no time."

She needed to be doing something productive to keep her mind away from the fact that there was something huge and mean trying to get in. The patchwork using the closet door wouldn't totally keep the cold out, but at least there would be some kind of barrier. A little something. Something was better than nothing, right? Right.

Mandy hurried out of the room, heart thrumming. The living room lamps flickered, but, thankfully, remained on. The power was still on and that was a definite plus.

The beast was quiet again. Maybe it got trapped under the collapsed chimney or maybe it was knocked out. Either was fine with her.

The two and a half inch screws and power screwdriver, what Grandma always called a drill, waited for her in a narrow cabinet near the back door. She checked to make sure the thing was charged.

A low growl rumbled through the door to her right. She switched the box of screws and power screwdriver to her left hand and drew her pistol with the right. She froze, listening.

Another growl filtered through the thick door. Both doors boasted a tiny three-inch by three-inch square window set about five feet up. Just enough to look through. A design for rangers to be able to get a feel for the outside before they stepped out. Just in case a bear was nearby or the weather was being crappy. Or, sometimes, a person just liked to stare out a window on a rainy day. Even if said window was about the size of a pack of cigarettes, give or take.

Mandy straightened, drew in a breath, and faced the back door. The square window was about eye level. All she needed to do was stand on her tiptoes a bit to look out.

The growl sounded again, this time a bit louder.

"What do you want?"

The only reply was another deep growl.

She turned away. It couldn't break down the doors. If it could, it would have already. She needed to get the windows patched up. If the generator ran out of gas, they would need all the patchwork in place to survive.

On the other hand, what if the creature on the other side of the door waited? What if it waited out the storm and the possible rescue only to rip them both apart as soon as one of the doors opened?

She turned to the back door, pistol still in hand, and rose onto her tiptoes to peer out the tiny window. Utter darkness greeted her for a moment until her vision adjusted. Yet, with all the wind and snow, she couldn't see much, so she flipped the backdoor light on...

...and gaped into the hazel eye of a beast.

A deep growl rose from the creature on the other side of the door. The very sound reverberated into her like the strum of a tuned-down bass guitar. It vibrated through her chest, stopping her heart for a second. The hazel eye narrowed, but before it did, Mandy thought she saw thin, black squiggles burrow through the white parts before disappearing. She frowned.

"What the fu—"

The monster roared, head tilting up to reveal large fangs.

Mandy stumbled away from the door, heart a wild mess, bladder heavy. She didn't know she needed to pee so bad until now.

The beast rammed the door, shaking it on its hinges. A shriek escaped her mouth and she tripped over her own feet, landing hard on her butt. She scooted away and the monster slammed into the door again. This time a sharp crack filled the cool air. Though nothing was visible, Mandy assumed it was an internal crack, which wasn't good either because the doors were reinforced with steel.

Then again, they were only designed to hold up against the onslaught of a large black bear and people meddling around, not the creature so hellbent on getting in right now. A creature so huge it was able to ram through a brick fireplace and chimney. Something large enough to crack steel inside a reinforced door.

"You okay?" Brett said, helping her to her feet.

"It's trying to break through the fucking door," she shouted.

Through the tiny square window, she stared at its hazel eye.

"It's watching us right now."

"Goddamn it," Brett said. "C'mon. Get your shotgun."

The beast bashed itself against the door again. This time it bowed toward her. Dozens of cracks bolted through the hardwood. It wasn't enough to create a gap around the edges, but enough to tell her she needed to get her ass in gear. She noted Brett still held the twelve-gauge.

"Stay here and shoot the fucker if I don't make it back in time."

Brett blinked. "Where the hell are you going?"

"Getting the four-ten," she said and thought about adding a "duh", but knew the guy was in a state of shock still. The cold and blizzard…now a monster trying to eat them. Yeah, she couldn't blame him for being a bit spacey right now. She was right there with him in some respects.

Her shotgun was on the bed. She swept it up and…

A sigh caught her attention. She glanced at the broken window, turned to leave, stopped and turned back.

Dark fingers capped with long, ragged nails slipped away from the inner frame of the window and disappeared into a flurry of snow.

It's following me, she thought.

But why? It didn't have a reason to. Unless seeing her through the tiny window in the door marked her in some way? She blinked. A swirl of snow blew through the window.

"Shit," she said.

"What?" Brett said behind her, and she about turned and blew his stupid head off.

Once her nerves calmed a bit, she said, "It saw me. Might have even smelled me."

"Okay? So?"

"So," she said. "It's hunting *me* now."

Brett didn't say anything for a handful of seconds. He moved toward the window and faced her. "So, what the hell are we supposed to do now? What's out there?"

"I don't know," she said, replying to both questions.

She stared at the broken window for an unknown amount of time. Maybe a minute, maybe more. "But we need to fight it."

Brett frowned. "Fight it? How—"

"Follow me."

BRETT

Baffled, he followed Mandy into the short hall and to the closed door at the end. She opened it quietly and motioned for him to step inside the room beyond.

He paused a moment, wondering if maybe, somehow, she realized why he was here or if she recognized him from before with the cigarette butt. Still, he stepped through the doorway into a pitch-black room. His right shin smacked something—the toilet, maybe—and he stumbled into something else. A sink? Pain flared up his leg and he limped to the side, tripped over a slight rise in the floor and would have fallen if his hand hadn't latched onto a towel rack, or handrail, or whatever the hell kept him from landing hard on his ass.

"Shh," she said, and the last bit of light snapped to complete darkness as the door closed.

"Hey, what—"

"Whisper," Mandy said. "I think it can hear us and understand what we're saying, too.

"I don't think it can hear us or smell me here."

"You mean," Brett said, "you hope it can't."

"Right. It's the best I got. Now, listen..."

He could do it now, he realized. Kill her. Just point the shotgun in the direction of her voice and pull the trigger. And he almost did. It would be one less thing to worry about and he might be able to trick the creature. If she was right and it was indeed hunting her now...he could hide, open a door, let it in and escape while it ate her. The blizzard would hurt like hell, but if he could find a good place to hide out until the cops came with the helicopter...

"The back door is about to give," Mandy whispered. "A couple of really good hits, and it will breach the cabin."

"Can it even get through the doorway, though?"

"I don't know." She paused for a few seconds. "Doesn't matter, though. Once it breaks through, and it will, we might as well let it eat us if we don't fight back because the generator won't be able to keep up with all that cold pumping in. We'll also need to figure out how to make a makeshift door."

"What about the cops?" Brett asked. "The helicopter? They'll be on their way eventually. If we kill it, we can just hole up in here where it'll be warm until they get here."

It made sense to him, but...

"You don't know the authorities around here, Brett. Oh, they'll be here, but it won't be until the storm completely dies down. That's just how they work."

He frowned. "But isn't it supposed to be settling down by now?"

"Does it sound like it's settling down?"

He listened to the howling wind for a moment and sighed. "Okay. Fine. So, it breaks down the door and we blast it to hell, or just stay here? I vote we just stay here."

"If we stay here, we're sitting ducks. We need to kill it first."

Why did she have to be so goddamn gung-ho? Her plan, which wasn't really a plan at all, was more dangerous than just chilling out in the bathroom until the cops arrive. They would be exposing themselves to—

A muffled crash broke through his thoughts.

"Shit," Mandy said.

"Shit? What do you mean 'shit'? What…"

"Shut up. I think it broke the back door down."

Brett's heart skipped a beat. She was right. They were sitting ducks in this tiny room. All it would have to do was tear the door off its hinges and reach in.

They stood silent for a long time. Brett wasn't sure how long. Felt like a goddamn hour, though. Finally, the swish of clothing filled the bathroom.

"Back me up," Mandy whispered.

"*What*?"

"I'm going to open the door and see if it's inside. I want you to stand behind me and back me up if you see anything. Just don't shoot me."

Brett snorted. Couldn't help it. Wasn't he thinking about doing just that not too long ago? Shooting her? Yes.

"You think this is funny?"

He blinked. "I—*no*. Sorry. Just stressed and scared." Not entirely a lie. But it was also funny in a sort of macabre way.

Brett shook his head, and, even though she couldn't see him, smiled his best smile. "Sorry. I laugh when I get scared or nervous."

"You pretty much already said that."

He grunted, nodding. *Fuck. You're losing it, man.*

She fell silent for a bit. Probably wondering why he was acting like an idiot. A suspicious idiot at this point.

Do it, a tiny yet familiar voice spoke up in his head. *Just point and pull the trigger.*

Then the bathroom door opened. Only a sliver. Enough for Mandy to peek through. He could just make out the profile of her face, neck, and chest. She didn't move for at least a minute and eventually blew out a heavy breath.

"Okay," she whispered. "Go to the back door. I'll drop to a knee so you'll have a clear shot too."

"Wait," he said, stopping her from opening the bathroom door fully. "What if it's waiting for us out there? Maybe it's in the living room or somewhere you can't see."

Highlighted by the outside of the bathroom, Mandy looked at him. "Then you better shoot it."

Brett frowned and Mandy swung the bathroom door open.

MANDY

The lamp in the living room flickered, giving the short hall and the way to the kitchen an eerie haunted house vibe.

She crept forward, shotgun pointed toward the kitchen, finger on the trigger. Ready to deliver hell to whatever might emerge around the corner. Cold air slithered along the sides of her sweaty face. Behind her came the soft, tentative steps of socked feet. Brett.

Brett…

Something was a tad off about him in the bathroom. The laugh, which, despite being nervous or scared when she let him in from the storm, was the first time he ever did so. A dead laugh, Grandma would have called it. No humor behind it. She understood he was scared, hell, so was she, but that laugh…

There was something going on with Brett and she wasn't fully sure she could trust him anymore. Not that she really did anyway, but still. He had been on the way to gaining some trust from her until the little laugh. That chuckle masked in the darkness of the bathroom. Somehow that unnerved her more than the beast trying to break in.

Or rather…the beast that had already broken in.

The wind bellowed. The cabin creaked and groaned around her. The air grew colder and colder the closer she got to the kitchen. Yeah, if the doorway couldn't be patched up, the generator might burn itself out. If that happened, things would go from terrifying to horrifying in a snap.

They had the satellite phone, but what good was that if rescue was impossible?

Then there was the monster lurking around…

Mandy stopped a couple of feet short of the kitchen. She stared at the refrigerator and tried to use its stainless-steel surface like a mirror to see if maybe the beast was nearby. But everything was too blurry, and she couldn't quite get the right angle.

Finally, she drew in a deep breath, blew it out slowly, and rounded the corner into the kitchen.

She almost fired a couple of slugs into the small snow drift creeping through the doorway. The kitchen was empty. Mandy's legs quivered and she backed away from the kitchen to sit down on the living room floor. Brett swung his twelve-gauge into the kitchen, paused, then lowered the gun. He straightened and sighed.

"We need to fix that, right?"

She had a few choice words she wanted to shout at him but stowed the rage. Barely. Instead, she said, "Uh, yeah. I already told you that."

"After killing the…well, whatever the fuck is out there," Brett said. "Yeah, I remember. So, should we try killing it now or board everything up? Because it's getting fuckin' cold in here."

Well, there was another change in the man. When had he been so assertive? Before, he seemed kind of meek. Not weak, just…not leadership material.

Unless it was all an act until now…

"Use the cupboard doors," she said. "Won't be perfect, but it might keep the—"

The front door burst open. Icy wind blasted her back and whipped her hair in all directions. A roar rose above the crashing of the door and the howling of the wind. A roar so loud it drowned everything else out. Even her thoughts.

Brett, face a perfect "O" of shock, backpedaled into the kitchen, slipped on a thin dusting of snow and fell hard on his back and the larger drift of snow near the open doorway. The shotgun clattered and slid toward the stove, about two feet away. Brett rolled onto his side, snow clinging to his dark hair. Once the roar eased, she heard him gasping for air. Guy got the wind knocked out of him.

A floorboard groaned behind her. A deep growl followed. The very same low rumbling, like a bass guitar strumming through her chest. She sat on the wooden planks of the floor, eyes wide, heart a galloping mess. She also had to pee really bad. A sensation just now pushing to the forefront for some damn reason.

The growl fell away as Brett, still gasping a bit, picked the twelve-gauge up and pointed it in Mandy's direction.

"Get down," he shouted.

She sprawled flat on the floor and Brett fired the shotgun. The brilliant boom of the gun immediately made Mandy's ears ring. She rolled away, clapping her hands to her ears a few seconds too late. All the ringing and rolling, it gave her an instant headache. She bumped into the debris of the collapsed chimney and shot a glance to the front door.

A swirl of snow blew through the open doorway, but other than that it was empty. On the floor and splattered near the doorway was a good amount of blood. Brett hit the target. But did he kill it? She tried to stand, but with all the ringing and pending migraine, she found a section of the couch to fall into. For the life of her, all she could do was sit on the couch and stare at the open doorway. The door itself, she noted in the vague, off-handed way one might notice an annoying bug on the wall, was missing.

Snow drifted across the threshold. Brett stood nearby, too. He was telling her something, or yelling, but she couldn't hear him through all the ringing. Instead, her gaze drifted back to the front doorway, the darkness, and what waited out there in the storm. Was it looking at her right now? Did Brett kill it?

Mandy crossed her arms and shivered while the sound of Brett's voice wavered through the ringing.

BRETT

Something was wrong with her.

No matter what he said she appeared not to hear a word and, for fuck's sake, it was frustrating. Because he needed to know where some tools might be so he could start boarding up the doorways. It was getting cold in the cabin now and it would only get colder.

She was supposed to get an electric screwdriver and some screws earlier but, so far, he hadn't been able to locate any of that. He stood on the line between the kitchen and living room and glanced back and forth at the doorways.

"Look," he said, hoping Mandy would respond. "I need to know where the screws and electric screwdriver are, okay? Not sure what the hell is wrong with you right now, but—"

"Did...did you kill it?" Mandy said in a trembling voice. It sounded so small. So...lost. It was the first time since the creature attacked she truly sounded terrified.

He didn't turn to look at her. Instead, he kept his eyes on the doorways. "I dunno. Maybe. A lot of blood on the floor and wall."

She was silent for a bit then said, "C-Cold."

"Yeah," he said. "You know where the screws and electric screwdriver are? I'll get started on boarding these doors up."

"I—I dropped them somewhere. Can't remember. Shit..." A minute or so crawled by. "Check near the back door. Kitchen area."

"Okay." Brett turned to the kitchen. He glanced around but didn't find anything. "You sure?"

"Yes," Mandy said without hesitation.

He didn't find anything near the fridge, or sink. He was little more than two feet from the open doorway when two things occurred to him simultaneously. The electric screwdriver was under a dusting of snow, and he crouched way too close to the open doorway. He blinked into the stormy night and all its swirling darkness.

Heart hammering, Brett grabbed the electric screwdriver and box of screws and backed away from the doorway.

Truth was, he didn't know if the thing was dead. It could be anywhere right now.

He returned to the living room to check on Mandy, who still sat on the couch, which must have moved after the fireplace and chimney were bashed in. He wasn't quite sure how. Maybe the force of all the bricks piling into the living room. Or, maybe, Mandy moved it at some point. She was gone for quite a while looking for the electric screwdriver before the monster tried breaking down the door, after all. Hell, he couldn't remember.

Too much going on for his brain to wrap around everything at once.

"Got the screwdriver and screws," he said.

Mandy blinked. She looked at him. "You saw it."

He sighed, nodding. "Yep. You want to help me with—"

"What did it look like?"

He glanced over his shoulder at the open front doorway. "I don't know. Big and hairy. Big teeth and claws."

"Claws?" She frowned. "Not hands?"

"Well, I mean, they kind of looked like both. I didn't exactly have time to take a bunch of mental pictures, you know."

Mandy nodded and her gaze lowered. "Right. Big and hairy?"

"Yeah. Like Bigfoot, or a really big ape of some kind. Maybe it's a deformed bear?"

She shook her head. "I think you got it right with the former."

His heart thudded. "What? Bigfoot?" He chuckled. "Bigfoot isn't real."

She smiled and looked at the open doorway. "I used to think so too."

Brett stared at her for a long time. *Just do it*, the old voice whispered in his head. *Just cut her up and make it look like a bear attack. Because that's what you saw. A deformed bear. Couldn't be Bigfoot. Bigfoot doesn't exist.*

Holding the electric screwdriver in his left hand, his right slipped into the pocket of his coat where the hunting knife greeted him. Brett's gaze remained on Mandy while his thumb unsnapped the strap around the handle of the knife. He shivered. His heart thrummed.

Just be quick, the small voice inside said. *Drag her body across the floor like a deformed bear*

91

would do. Throw her corpse outside and get these doorways boarded up.

He drew in a breath and gripped the handle of the knife in his right hand. He pulled it out of the sheath and…

Mandy perked up a bit. "You hear that?" She wasn't looking at him, but the doorway.

Brett blinked, shivered and cleared his throat. "W-What?"

She stood, rushed toward the door and skidded to a stop about four feet from it. She gaped out the doorway. "It's the helicopter!"

Brett's hand unfurled from the knife in his coat pocket, dropped the screwdriver and screws and grabbed his shotgun. He joined her, though didn't hear anything. At least she still had her shotgun.

"I don't hear anything," Brett said, after a minute or so.

"The wind shifted," Mandy said. "Hold on."

Brett stepped closer to the doorway. About a foot away, maybe less. He frowned into the night and the sheets of snow and frigid gusts of wind. He still didn't hear anything.

A light swept by the front of the cabin, barely cutting through the snowy gusts of wind. Wind which switched directions and…

He heard it. The wup-wup-wup-wup of a helicopter. Brett's heart tripped over itself.

"They're here," he said. "They made it." He turned to Mandy, but she was already slipping on her boots and parka.

"I know. Get your boots on. We're blowing this popsicle stand."

"In the cabin," a voice boomed. "We're only able to keep it steady for a few minutes at a time. We will lower a basket down. Please get inside and buckle the harness. Our visibility is near zero so you have three minutes from the time the basket is lowered to get in."

Mandy gave him a push. "Get your boots on."

Brett blinked, thought about blowing her head off, but instead did as he was told. Lacing up his boots, he concluded he would not kill her. This brought a slight wave of relief, despite what the murderous little voice inside wanted him to do and its disappointment. That bastard was never satisfied, though.

"We are lowering the basket now," the man from the helicopter boomed.

Brett stood, grabbed the twelve-gauge and met Mandy outside the doorway.

MANDY

She didn't expect them to be here yet. Especially since the storm was still raging. Still, they made it and she wouldn't let the opportunity slip.

They couldn't stay in the cabin anymore. The damage was too much and if the monster, Bigfoot, whatever, was still around, it would eventually get them. Better to cut their losses and get the hell out.

Besides, if the lost hunters were still out there, she doubted they were still alive now. Especially if they crossed paths with the creature. She hoped they found a place to hole up for the night, though. Maybe one of them was a survivalist and could get them tucked into a nice hollow or shallow limestone cave. Maybe they got a small fire going. All in all, she hoped they were okay and would return to the cabin in a couple of days with Ron.

The cabin needed serious repairs and Ron was a Jack of All Trades if ever there was one.

No one could have predicted a Bigfoot, or whatever, attacking the cabin and practically destroying it. With Brett as a witness, even Ed would have to believe her. She's never lied on the job and tried not to make it a habit outside of it.

The basket banged against the roof of the cabin, bounced away and swung like a possessed pendulum before finally breaking through the snow and slamming onto the ground about ten feet from the front stoop.

"Go ahead," Brett said.

She almost laughed in his face and pushed him toward the basket. "I'm with the Forest Service, so, no, you go ahead." And when he frowned at her, she added, "Part of the job. Stow your masculinity for a few minutes and just get in the basket. Not much time now."

As if they could hear, the man in the helicopter said, "You have less than two minutes to enter the basket and buckle in."

Brett nodded, smiled, and patted her shoulder. She smiled back. He ran to the rescue basket hunched over against the warring winds and cascading snow. After that, she lost visual of him for a few seconds while the winds shifted again.

"We are lifting the basket now," the man on the helicopter boomed. "Secure yourself."

By the time the winds died down, Brett was already in the air. He didn't appear to be buckled in, but still held onto the twelve-gauge she gave him. He swayed a bit, but nothing horrible and soon disappeared through the swirling snow above. She just thanked whatever gods there were that the cabin rested in thick forest. If it had been out in the open or with just a few trees around, there would be no rescue helicopter. It wouldn't have even been a thought. It still surprised her they tried it anyway. Trees or no trees.

Relief spilled through Mandy. She smiled and glanced behind her to see if she forgot—

A roar cut through the noise of the helicopter. Her heart stuttered and she turned back to the outside just in time to catch a massive creature rush by and leap into the stormy snow.

She gasped, stumbled back into the cabin, and caught herself before falling on her butt.

She thought she heard someone scream. Someone else shouted something. Was that a gunshot? The helicopter noise grew louder and...

The wind shifted again, blinding her from anything outside the doorway and deafening her to any sounds. The howling of the wind and snow blasting into the cabin was all she knew for a few minutes.

Still, even through all of that, she could have sworn she heard a loud crash. Crunching metal. More screaming.

But she couldn't be sure.

Mandy, shivering, backed away from the doorway while the storm raged and cold blasted its way in.

BRETT

There was no way to stop it.

The monster burst through the snow and grappled onto the side of the basket with one of its large hands. A couple of long fingernails sliced through the thigh of his jeans. He cried out and tried to reposition himself so he could blow the fucking thing's head off with his shotgun.

But the beast latched on with both hands and shook the basket so hard it knocked the gun from Brett's grip. It fell into his lap, the barrel sticking through one of the basket's steel diamond-shaped holes.

"Hold on," the man from the helicopter shouted. "There must be some turbulence...holy *shit*!"

Holy shit is right, Brett thought when they pointed the spotlight directly on the basket and the monster dangling from it.

With all the light on it, he saw its face...its teeth and dark, bloodshot eyes rolling back and forth in their sockets. And...he could have sworn something black squiggled in the whites. Like tiny worms, but then the light moved, shrouding the creature in relative darkness.

"You, in the basket," the man from the helicopter shouted. "Hold on! We need to stabilize."

Stabilize? How far up was he? Couldn't be too far, right? If the monster jumped it. Maybe twenty-five feet? Maybe less? More? He couldn't rationalize anything over twenty-five, though. As big as the creature was, surely it couldn't jump higher than that.

Right?

The beast roared and shook the cage again. It swung back and forth, taking Brett and the basket with it for a vomit inducing ride.

"You in the basket," the man in the helicopter shouted through what Brett assumed was a bullhorn. "Remain still. We cannot stabilize if you are swinging the basket."

"It's the fucking Bigfoot trying to kill me, jackass," Brett shouted back, but the man probably couldn't hear him over the noise of the helicopter.

The wind picked up. Snow pelted his exposed face at every turn, making it hard to breathe. Every so often, he caught glimpses of the monster still clinging to the cage, its teeth bared. The madness in its wide eyes. Still, it swung him and the basket back and forth. Each pass seemed to get wider and wider and with it, the helicopter made loud revving noises. To compensate for the weight changes, Brett assumed. The poor pilot was probably ready to cut the basket loose and get the hell out of the area.

The monster roared and reached out for Brett. He pulled his shotgun free and pointed it at the creature.

Everything was dashed away in a sheet of snow, blinding him before he could pull the trigger.

"Fuck." He tried to shield himself from the icy onslaught with an arm, accidentally dropping the shotgun again.

When the wind subsided, the monster wasn't there.

Brett coughed, heart tumbling over itself, and looked around for the gun. It wasn't on his lap or in the basket. He glanced toward the ground and sighed. Great. Now he was unarmed, and the beast was still out there somewhere. Maybe it decided Mandy was the easier meal option. Maybe it's in the cabin and tearing her apart right now.

Something heavy fell onto the basket and, at first, Brett wasn't sure if the wailing thing clinging to the metal rescue basket was human or not. Then it scrambled closer, reaching out for him. Brett was about to punch the thing, then stopped as the light of the helicopter swung over the basket. Brett grimaced. His stomach churned.

A man, yes, but most of his face was torn off and the rest of his head was in bloody tatters. The skin, anyway. The man's face was a wailing hole with teeth and bulging eyes. Somehow the creature leapt from the basket to the helicopter. Or did it just climb really fast?

Brett grabbed the injured man's hand and—

A tremendous roar blasted through the wind and noise of the helicopter.

Brett glanced up in time to see the helicopter swerve drastically away from the cabin. The basket swung around in a quick arc and Brett lost his grip and the wailing man slipped away from the basket, swallowed up by the storm below.

"Shit!" Brett gripped the sides of the basket while the helicopter dipped, rose, sliced back and forth, then began to spin like a demented carnival ride.

Snow blasted into him from what seemed like every direction, blinding him. Something somewhere was beeping. Someone screamed. At least it sounded like someone screamed. Brett couldn't be sure. The world was blind, spinning madness. At one point the vomit burst from his mouth. At another, he began to sob. He just wanted it to end. Please, God, let it stop.

It was as if God was listening…

Brett soon became aware of two things: A harsh crunching noise and the drastic sense of falling.

He sucked in a breath as a sudden jolt struck the basket and a wave of snow gobbled him up.

Then everything went dark.

***

The wind had died down some so he decided to venture out of the deep hollow and find better shelter. He wasn't in his territory and hoped the storm would mask his scent enough to pass through without alerting the alpha in the area.

He was too young to battle a mature alpha and he knew it.

All he wanted to do was pass through and head farther north where there weren't so many people. Or outlings, as some called them. Those with great intelligence yet could be very vile creatures if they chose to be. They were best to be avoided at all costs.

The moment he emerged from the hollow, he caught the whiff of smoke on the air. Air which was getting colder and still swirling with snow.

He took a few steps in the direction of the smoke scent when a loud crashing noise sent him stumbling back. Not far, what might be fire blazed through the trees. So, maybe he hadn't been dreaming when he heard strange unnatural noises in the forest. The wup-wup-wup sound of a giant bird the outlings rode on was especially worrisome. Sometimes they rode that loud bird over the forests, and it always scared him.

The wup-wup-wup was gone though, so maybe it was just a dream? And what was the loud crashing noise? Why was there fire?

The breeze shifted and he got a full assault of scents. Mainly smoke but there was something else too. Something...sick...

The stench of bad blood.

Of extreme illness.

But not the blood of an outling. No, this was different.

A frown creased his broad forehead. He drew in a few more breaths of the smoke and blood.

Curious, he started forward.

Something screamed. An outling? If so, maybe it was better to continue his journey north and let it all be. Best to not come in contact with people.

He began to do just that when another much stronger whiff of the bad blood scent snagged his attention. It stank like something rotten. Fish left in the sun too long came to mind. He huffed out a loud and heavy breath. He should ignore it all and keep moving.

His gaze returned to the glow of the fire through the trees and, eventually, curiosity won.

MANDY

The basket with Brett still inside swung by the front of the cabin more than twice before the helicopter made a harsh grinding noise and dropped out of the sky about ten feet from her stoop.

The blast of snow sent her stumbling backward. She ducked behind the couch and waited for the surge of snow and dirt, and whatever else was flying through the open doorway, to subside. Something heavy struck the other side of the couch and thumped on the floor. Once everything quieted down, Mandy peeked over the top of the couch at the doorway.

She couldn't stop shivering. The cold was getting to her. Not even her parka was helping much now.

The doorway was empty, giving way only to the icy darkness of the night.

The helicopter crashed, but where was Brett? Did he manage to get out and away before it all came down? Or...or...

She hadn't known the man for more than a few hours, but she still cared. She still wanted him to live. Even if he gave off weird vibes every now and then.

Mandy stood. A thin veil of snow swirled through the doorway. The drift appeared to be at least knee-high. She glanced behind her toward the kitchen, sure some hulking beast with blood matted fur and a mouthful of teeth would be standing there.

But the kitchen was empty. She still carried the four-ten shotgun and a quick look around for the twenty-gauge proved useless. Would the four-ten have enough stopping power? She might have made a mistake choosing that over the twenty-gauge. Maybe…

Slowly, she stepped around the couch and moved toward the front doorway, shotgun ready. She spared another glance at the kitchen. Nothing. She continued moving toward the front doorway, body quaking with shivers. Not entirely from the cold, but fear too. Where was the monster? Hiding somewhere, waiting. But where? The shivering made everything ache.

She stopped at the knee-high drift before the doorway and tried to see outside. All was darkness with whisps of swirling white snow, however, so she swallowed down a hard lump in her throat, glanced behind her quickly, then stepped through the drift to the threshold.

The wind hissed and howled around the cabin. Snow sprinkled her face. Mandy turned away, shivering. She couldn't do it. She…

Her gaze fell on an object at the foot of the couch.

It only took her another couple of seconds to realize the object was a severed head. The face was too mangled for her to tell if it was Brett or not. Strong shivers battered her body. Nevertheless, she faced the doorway once more.

A scream pierced the wind. A second or two, then gone.

Mandy frowned and stepped to the doorway again. Merely a foot away, she leaned forward, trying to listen for the scream. Maybe it was Brett. Maybe he had a broken leg or was hurt really bad from the crash and needed her to help.

Another scream cut through the howling of the wind.

She was about to rush out into the storm to find Brett when a deep, rumbling growl rose behind her.

BRETT

Someone screamed, but it was a distant sound. Nothing to worry about.

Brett floated somewhere between reality and the dreamworld. A place where dreams and reality clashed. He was pushing his kid on the swing, but the location was skewed...changed. Instead of the backyard, they were in the old motel room where he slit the throat of Liv Banner. One of his first murders. His kid swung above the corpse, little legs pumping and shouting at him to, "go higher". He pushed harder and harder and, in the distance, someone was screaming. Still, he pushed and pushed and—

Everything melded back to reality. Brett sat in the metal rescue basket, shivering from the cold. He tried opening his eyes beyond squints, but the world still spun like a top so he clamped them shut again, which didn't help either. Hot saliva filled his mouth. His throat constricted. His stomach roiled. There was no time to turn.

Brett glutted vomit down his chest and into his lap.

The screaming grew louder and louder. Was the person getting closer or had his mind finally cracked? What if he was trapped in some horrifying nightmare? What if he was really in a coma and this would be his world until whoever out there pulled the plug...or he woke up?

And still, the screaming got louder and louder.

It was like the person screaming stood right beside the rescue basket. Leaning over Brett and just wailing into his ear.

His eyes opened little by little and still squinted due to the intense winds and sheets of snow.

The screaming was so loud, though, he barely heard the wind.

Everything hurt. The skin on his exposed face was numb. Especially his nose. Not a good sign. If he didn't get somewhere warm soon, frostbite would...

Brett glanced to the right and his eyes widened, despite how they felt like they were sheathed in ice.

A man's screaming face levitated inches from his own.

Brett tried to get away, but even though he wasn't strapped in, he couldn't get away from the screaming man. Couldn't escape the basket.

The screaming man gripped the side of the basket, body quaking, highlighted by the glow from the cabin. He shook the basket, though nothing like what the monster had done.

The monster...

Where was it?

"Hey," Brett shouted as the wind subsided. "Hey, you're okay."

The man, voice hoarse and strained, eyes nearly bulging, shook his head. Eventually, however, the screaming melted to harsh sobs. He buckled beside the basket, shivering and crying.

Brett, wincing at all the bumps and bruises, cuts and aches, stood in the basket. He glanced at the man leaning against the basket. The pilot, no doubt.

The other man had most of his face torn off. Brett thought about strangling him. Save the man from lifelong trauma. Just throttle the guy until…

Then, from inside the cabin, Mandy screamed.

A shotgun blast followed.

MANDY

The creature was so massive that even when it hunched over, its shoulders and the back of its head scraped the seven-foot ceiling.

She screamed with both shock and terror. How did it sneak up so quickly? And how the hell was it so quiet? The thing was *huge*. How…

The beast glared at her with wide eyes. Eyes that didn't look quite right. Black squiggles squirmed throughout the whites. A runner of what appeared to be green snot dangled from one of its ape-like nostrils. A deep rattling sound came from its broad chest.

Walking backwards, the back of her knees struck the couch and she plopped down. A small gasp escaped her. Mandy stared at the monster looming over her, large, yellow teeth bared. Long claws splayed and ready to rip her apart. She pointed the shotgun at the creature.

It lunged and she pulled the trigger of the four-ten.

The boom in such a small space immediately made her deaf. Only high-pitched ringing followed. Gun smoke obscured her vision for a moment or two, then she saw the monster staggering toward the front doorway. One of its arms held snug against its stomach. It dropped to its knees for a bit, head lowered. Blood dripped onto the small snow drift by the door, turning the white scarlet.

Temporarily (at least she hoped it was only temporary) deaf or not, she wasn't going to let it escape into the storm where it could gain the upper hand again.

She stood from the couch and pointed the four-ten at the beast and—

A large, dark hand gripped the barrel of the shotgun and yanked it out of her grip before she could pull the trigger.

Mandy stumbled away and drew her pistol, but it was slapped out of her hand with tremendous force.

She tripped over her own feet and fell hard on her butt.

Just as gigantic as the one she shot, another Bigfoot hunched over her. Was it a Bigfoot? The name was the only thing that made sense to her brain right now. She closed her eyes, bracing for whatever horrors it was about to inflict on her and the pain that would rule her world until she died.

But when nothing happened, she opened her eyes and stared at the beast. It still stood over her. Still just as huge and menacing as the other, except...

Except their eyes, hell their entire demeanor was different. There were no black squiggles in the whites of this creature. Rather, its gaze appeared solemn...sad. She didn't see madness, but intelligence in those eyes. And unlike the other one she shot, it appeared concerned for her. Nonthreatening.

As her hearing gradually returned, she thought she even heard it whining deep in its throat. Like a sad, distressed, or injured dog might sound. Only deeper. Maybe a sound a great ape might make. Maybe not. Her mind shot off into so many directions, she couldn't harness them all.

It reached out an immense hand and Mandy recoiled.

A low sigh filtered through its nostrils and it cocked its head to the side, as if trying to understand why she was so scared. Then its eyes widened slightly. It looked away, glancing over its shoulder at the other creature. Its hazel eyes held on her for a long time and in that minute, or so, she understood. Through its gentle gaze and soft whining. She knew, hell, she *felt*, the beast meant her no harm and the one that attacked her was different. Sick or insane. Or both. Maybe this Bigfoot caught the scent of bad blood? Maybe it was curious and decided to check things out.

Mandy's nerves eased a bit, beginning to understand—

A muffled thump and a section just below the sternum of the new Bigfoot suddenly bulged outward. Like something was trying to get out.

Mandy blinked.

The Bigfoot also blinked and glanced down at itself. Its mouth opened in something she recognized as shock. Wide-eyed. Terrified, yet confused.

A deep growl gurgled from somewhere behind the creature standing over her followed by a harsh sucking sound. The beast jerked, swayed a bit. Tears trickled from those wide, trembling eyes down its cheeks. A strained moan escaped its open mouth.

Thud.

A huge fist burst through the beast's stomach, splattering Mandy in blood. She screamed, scrambled to her feet, and tripped over the scattered bricks of the ruined fireplace, landing hard on her butt again.

The dying Bigfoot made a strangled gagging sound. Loops of intestines dangled out of its abdomen like dead gray snakes. It dropped to its fur-covered knees. Its gaze fixed on Mandy for a few seconds. A long gush of air blew from its mouth, and it fell face first onto the ruins of the fireplace, giving way to the monster in the cabin.

It growled, picked the dead Bigfoot up and tossed it aside. The body crashed into the couch, collapsing it, and rolled into the wall.

Mandy was blood streaked, body quaking from the cold and the monster's toothy snarl. She didn't have a gun. Blood streamed from a hole in the right side of the creature's chest. She glanced around for anything she might use as a weapon. Hell, even the fire poker would be better than nothing. The only objects close enough, though, were bricks. She scooped one up and threw it at the monster.

It bounced off its broad chest and thumped to the floor.

The Bigfoot huffed and lumbered closer to Mandy.

She threw another brick. And another. Another. She cried out in rage and pain and terror. She shrieked at the thing. This nightmare beast from out

THE CABIN

of the storm. She wailed. She threw bricks. She spat at it.

And still, the monster moved closer and closer. A low, very deep growl rumbled in its thick throat.

Its massive claw reached out for her...

"Get away from her, you son of a bitch."

It paused, blinked. Its gorilla-like nostrils flared, as if taking in a scent. Its sloping brow furrowed, and it straightened as best it could under the shorter ceiling.

Before Mandy could move, a claw grabbed her by the forearm and swung her around with it. The grip on her arm was so strong she cried out from the pain and kicked at the beast. She might die, but she would do so fighting.

"Ah, hell, you're uglier than I thought."

She glanced toward the front door and her heart stuttered.

Brett, his parka torn in places and a cut on his forehead still streaming blood, pointed his twelve-gauge in her and the monster's direction.

The growls emanating from the creature were constant and maddening. The grip on her arm tightened and she sucked a sharp breath in through clenched teeth from the pain.

Brett stepped closer, cocking an eyebrow. "Your move, Hoss."

Mandy kicked at the creature and tried to pry her arm out of its grip. One of her feet swung high and clocked the monster under the chin hard enough for its grip to loosen and drop her. She hit the floor and rolled away, heart a harried mess.

"Hey," Brett said, regaining the monster's attention. "Dumbass." He grunted and kept the shotgun aimed at the Bigfoot. "Oh, yeah. You remember me, don't ya."

The creature's growl deepened.

Mandy crept toward the hall. If she could get to the kitchen, maybe she'd find the twenty-gauge. The four-ten might be in the same area too. She didn't see it while sneaking behind the monster, nor her pistol.

Brett stepped closer to the beast. "Say goodbye, you ugly motherfucker."

Mandy slipped into the hall just as the monster began to roar.

BRETT

As soon as Mandy made it into the hall the beast roared so loud Brett's ears rang.

It rushed forward and Brett pulled the twelve-gauge's trigger.

The boom was about as deafening as the monster's roar. He didn't see where the shot hit the creature, but the force was enough to swing it back and away from Brett. He glanced to his right in time to see Mandy sifting through snow and other debris. Looking for a gun?

He glanced around, spotted her pistol a couple of feet away, and kicked it toward the kitchen. He didn't know if she got it or not because the monster was looking at him again. It stood, left shoulder leaking blood. A hunched monster with wide, dark eyes. The eyes of madness.

Brett didn't know if it was sick or just plain evil and really it didn't matter. What mattered was killing the bastard before it tore him to pieces like the other guy. The screaming pilot was out there somewhere, still. Maybe still sobbing and clinging to the rescue basket. Maybe wandering around in the blizzardy forest, screaming into the icy winds. Maybe madness stole what was left of his reason and he was out there running about in the woods naked.

The monster lunged and Brett pulled the trigger of his shotgun.

It moved too fast to get any aim, the shot striking it in the right leg.

It yelped, but already gained so much momentum the shotgun blast did near to nothing at stopping its progress. The creature yanked the gun from his hands and smacked him across the face so hard everything went bright white and he knew no more.

MANDY

She picked the pistol up in time to see the creature slam into Brett and strike him with a massive slap to the head before it collapsed, whining deep in its throat.

It rolled onto its side...facing Mandy.

She blinked, frozen by the monster's cold stare.

It bared blood-stained teeth at her, growled and rolled onto its stomach. The beast coughed up a glob of what might be mucus and blood onto the floor and reached out, huge claw splayed. She scooted backward and aimed the pistol at its face.

"Don't move," she shouted.

But it didn't appear to understand. The monster brought the claw down, nails digging into the wooden floor and pulled itself closer to her.

Mandy gasped, stood, spun to the back door, tripped over something but kept her balance. She was about to run to the doorway when something sharp slashed her ankle. She cried out, stumbled and fell into the knee-high drift of snow creeping in through the open door. Agony surged up her right leg. Teeth gritted, she pulled herself through the cold snow.

A large hand, claw, whatever the hell it was considered on a Bigfoot, snared her left ankle. A deep growl cut through all the pain, the thundering of her own heart. She glanced back just as the monster pulled her closer.

"*No.*" She flailed and clawed through the snow with her free hand. She tried kicking it in the face, but her right leg wouldn't work like she wanted it to and missed. The very act of moving it sent nauseating waves of agony through her.

It pulled her closer, dragging her through the snow and back onto the hardwood floor. The pressure gripping her left ankle ground the bones together, sparking more agony.

Its large teeth snapped, as if in anticipation. As if it couldn't wait to taste her flesh. Maybe that's what it wanted all along. Maybe it just wanted to eat her and everyone else was getting in the way. No. The more she got to see of its eyes, the tiny black squiggles in the whites, she knew it was sick. An illness altering its behavior. Something—

The monster gave a tremendous yank, dragging her the rest of the way, and bit down on her boot-clad left foot. Teeth punctured the boot and found skin. What if whatever it was infected with could be transferred with a bite? What if…

Mandy turned as best she could and pointed the pistol at the monster's face. Its mouth opened, releasing her foot and blinked at her.

"Get fucked."

She squeezed the trigger.

The monster's right eye disappeared in a splatter of blood and bone and dark brown fur. The beast howled, released her leg and rolled onto its back, hands clasped to its face.

Mandy, both legs injured now, crawled through the back doorway and into the remnants of the blizzard. The wind settled and the snow sifted down like fine powder. The air, however, was like falling into an icy lake. It took the breath right out of her.

She gasped and turned around so her face was free of the falling snow until she caught her breath again. She wasn't wearing gloves and every time she lifted them from the snow, they grew more and more numb. The shed housed the generator, about twenty feet from the cabin.

Twenty feet, she thought. *Not too far. It'll be warmer in there.*

Mandy turned in the direction of the shed, spotted it through the sifting snow, and began crawling towards it, pistol still in hand.

BRETT

Loud howling and roaring noises drew Brett back from the white silence he was suspended in for...well, for however long it had been.

He opened his eyes, groaned at the flickering lights in the living room, closed his eyes, and rolled onto his side. His head...it was like twenty rubber hammers pummeling simultaneously.

Very close, a monster howled.

At first, he didn't know why there was a monster or why it was howling. Or, if it was even real. Hell, he didn't even know where he was right now. Pain laced his head. His entire body trembled and ached. Cold.

Why am I so cold?

But he didn't dare open his eyes yet. His head hurt too much. His eyes, fuck, his eyes might as well be jelly right now. He didn't want to move, let alone think. Yet, his mind refused to stop. Images shuffled through.

Here...The disgusted face of a woman in a green parka.

Here...The same woman, but she was smiling slightly this time and sitting on a couch by a fireplace.

Now...A hulking beast leaping through the snow and...

Brett gasped and opened his eyes to a huge mound of what appeared to be brown fur dragging itself through an open doorway.

It took only a moment for the rest to click into place.

A Bigfoot was trying to kill them, and he'd been knocked out. He couldn't remember how he got knocked out, but sure as shit…it happened. Brett found his twelve-gauge and turned toward the large brown mound squeezing through the doorway leaving a thick trail of blood in its wake.

The beast was hurt bad. Good.

Still a bit disoriented, he glanced around for Mandy, but didn't see her. Probably for the best. Shit went south fast after arriving at the cabin. He hated himself for even following her here. Should have just let it go and spent the downtime with his kid. And for roughly the hundredth time in the last few hours, he thought about just leaving. Slip out of the cabin and through the woods back into town. Would it be one hell of a trek? Yep. Would his chances of survival double?

Maybe.

He looked at the front doorway and started moving toward it, then the monster whined from the opposite side of the cabin. Brett stopped, sighed, and faced the beast. It was trapped in the doorway for a few seconds, then turned a bit and squirmed through, sliding into the snow outside.

He frowned. Was it trying to get away or…?

Brett spared another glance around. Mandy was missing. It was hurt worse than before. So, she must have shot it again after the light went out. So, where was she?

The monster pulled itself out of view.

The wind had died down, leaving the world around the cabin eerily silent. His heart hammered. He swallowed a hard lump in his throat. It was so quiet he heard the click his dry throat made. Too goddamn quiet.

"Fuck," he whispered and took a few steps toward the back door.

He stopped and turned to the front door.

After a couple of seconds, he hurried through the front doorway, away from the monster, before his mind could stop him.

MANDY

The generator's shed was two things as she opened the door and crawled inside.

Instant warmth and a welcoming chugging sound. She forgot the generator also heated the shed enough to keep things from freezing up. Most notably, the well, its pump, and piping. Newfangled thermal rings ran along the pipe running to the cabin to keep it from freezing for running water.

The walls, pretty much everything in the shed, were soundproofed so not to scare or traumatize wildlife. Worked perfectly. She didn't even hear the chugging of the generator until she got to the door. And even then, it was faint.

Once inside she locked the door from the inside and rolled onto her back and released a breath too heavy to be a sigh. Something that was almost a sob.

She hoped the monster was dead. Or, if it wasn't, it had crawled off into the woods to do so.

She wondered about Brett, but knew he got knocked out, so he wasn't a main priority. If they were lucky, he'd be unconscious until the creature was gone…or dead. It killed one of the helicopter crew. How many were out there now still alive? How many died in the crash?

Mandy shivered and focused on getting herself warm first. Being able to feel her hands was a priority. She needed to know her physical capabilities before doing anything else. Luckily the industrial generator also powered a low wattage yellow bulb for her to see by. She shimmied closer to the heater output of the generator, hands bright red from the cold, and held them in front of the vent. It wouldn't surprise her if she got frostbite out there. Even in the small amount of time she was fully exposed. Maybe—

A gush of frigid air burst through the shed.

Mandy sucked in a sharp breath as if she'd been slapped and rolled onto her side to see the monster clawing its way across the shed's threshold. It appeared the right eye, along with a small portion of its head, was a mangled splatter of gore. In the dim, yellow light, however, she wasn't one hundred percent sure. Could be just blood-matted fur hanging over its eye.

I hurt it, Mandy thought. *There's no way it still has an eye after that shot.*

Still, she decided to face the creature like it had both eyes and its vision unburdened.

Its visible eyes shifted back and forth until it spotted her. Deep gurgling came from the monster. Not quite a growl. The Bigfoot grunted while it pulled itself farther into the shed. About mid-torso deep.

The shed was twenty-five feet long by twenty feet wide with the generator itself sitting roughly fifteen feet from the door. The monster was easily over seven feet tall. Its arms were long, meaning she only had a few seconds before it clawed the rest of the way to her.

Mandy, holding onto the generator, lifted herself up into a sitting position. She glanced behind her, but the only things at the back of the shed were maintenance tools and supplies, a bunch of five-gallon gas cans, and a riding lawnmower.

She returned her attention to the monster, which had already gained another three or four feet closer to her. Her heart slammed. Her stomach churned and she choked down vomit threatening to erupt from her mouth. Her entire body quaked with shivers. Hands burning from the exposure to extreme cold, trembling, Mandy somehow managed to lift the pistol and point it at the monster.

BRETT

By the cabin's flickering lights, he watched the creature drag itself into the shed not far from the side of the cabin.

Brett, fighting the intense cold eating at the exposed skin of his face and hands, shook his head and turned to the smoldering ruination of the helicopter and Mandy's SUV. He knew he might have to walk back to town but thought the SUV might have been spared in the crash when he limped by it to the cabin where he found another monster, dead, and the one that attacked them going for Mandy. A second look at the damage, though, proved he'd indeed be walking his ass through the snow and cold.

Or...he could kill the motherfucking thing, kill Mandy, and board up the cabin until spring or a nice warm up to make his hike back to town.

Only issue with that plan was cops had already been called. When the helicopter didn't report back, they'd send more cops. Which might be soon. If he shot Mandy, they'd get him on murder.

But...but if he let it kill her and then blew its ugly head off...

Yes. Now there was an option. He could play the lost hiker thing up. Mandy took him in during the storm and the monster attacked them. It took out the helicopter, broke into the cabin, knocked him out, and dragged her to the shed to kill her. It was wounded bad so he would tell the cops Mandy was the one who deserved the credit for being a hero. She saved him a couple of times. Then, when he came to, he found them in the shed, the beast barely alive, and he killed it.

There was no way they could debunk the story and they wouldn't have found his latest killing near town before all these events transpired anyway. He'd walk away a free man without suspicion, especially with the evidence of not one but two goddamn Bigfoot creatures in the vicinity and return to his kiddo. And that would be that.

There was just one problem; even though he came here to kill Mandy in the first place, the urge had passed. Well, for the most part anyway. The maddening need to kill her had dissipated. He didn't know why, but he kind of liked her. Not like a friend, but...he admired her strength. And, after only a few hours of knowing her, he respected her. Not that she needed his respect or anything. There wasn't a need to kill her anymore.

Or let her be killed.

Brett watched the monster's large feet slip inside and glanced over his shoulder at the snow-covered road leading away from the cabin.

MANDY

"Go away," Mandy said, still pointing the gun at the monster as it continued to pull itself closer and closer. "Just go away."

The Bigfoot's bloody upper lip curled in what appeared to be a grin, revealing long, jagged teeth.

It was almost fully inside the shed now. Its one-eyed glare never faltered from her.

Yet, the closer it got, the more she saw and the more her heart sank a little. There were indeed thick strands of blood-laden fur obscuring the right eye for when it moved its head a bit, she caught the glimmer from the low watt lightbulb. Instead of hitting the eye, which explained how it survived the pointblank shot, the round struck the thick brow bone above the eye. Enough to hurt like hell and crack its skull a bit, but kill it?

Not so much.

Its giant feet scooted across the wooden threshold and the doors clapped shut.

About five feet away now, give or take, and it was still coming.

Wet slurping sounds floated out of the monster's mouth.

"Stop," Mandy said in a strangled voice. "Please, just stop."

But the monster did not stop.

The monster would not stop.

The monster wanted blood and it intended to have it.

Hands burning from the severe cold, trembling, Mandy aimed the pistol the best she could at the left eye, the one most visible.

Its ragged fingernails clawed at the wooden planks and dragged itself closer.

Her finger slowly squeezed the trig—

The shed doors flew open. A burp of bitter cold air and snow struck her. Mandy turned away to avoid the snow and when she looked back, Brett stood in the doorway, twelve-gauge pointed at the monster.

The creature gasped, bared its blood-stained teeth in what might be pain and glanced behind it. A deep growl shook the floor.

"You okay?" Brett glanced at Mandy.

"I was about to kill it."

Brett nodded and took a step inside the shed. "Better back up. This might get messy."

"A twelve-gauge that close is going to do more than make a mess," Mandy said. "You even know how to aim it?"

He frowned at her. "What the fuck is that supposed to—"

The monster rolled, kicking Brett's feet out from under him. The shotgun went off, slug striking the generator. The light stuttered, flickered, though remained on. The creature was on top of Brett before he could scream.

Mandy rose to her knees, agony gripping her legs and aimed the pistol at the back of the Bigfoot's head. Before she could pull the trigger, it buried its teeth into the side of Brett's neck. Brett shrieked and tried to punch and kick his way out from under the monster, but its weight was too great. It had him pinned. Blood squirted and misted the icy air as it tore into him.

Choking back a sob, Mandy crawled over to the mountain of monster and pressed the muzzle of her pistol on the back of its head.

Her gaze shifted to Brett's wide, terrified eyes.

"I'm sorry," she said, and squeezed the trigger.

A small glut of blood and skull fragments splashed her hand and forearm, but Brett's face was a horror show. Blood, bits of brain and bone...

He didn't move.

Even when she managed to roll the monster off him, he didn't move. It only took her another few seconds to realize the hole in his right temple. The monster's bite would have killed him, but her bullet gave him a quicker, less painful way out.

She sat in the shed staring at the dead creature for a long time. So long, she forgot where she was until dawn's light filtered through the trees, giving all the freshly fallen snow the glimmer of tiny diamonds.

Mandy blinked and her gaze drifted to the outside.

Her entire body hurt. The cold was almost unbearable.

Using what little strength she had, she rolled both bodies out into the snow and closed the shed's doors. The slug Brett fired, thankfully, didn't hit a vital part of the generator, but rather a support bar.

Mandy didn't know how much gas was in the generator and at the same time didn't care. It was over. Her body was shutting down.

Too much.

Too much stress.

Too much pain.

Too much blood.

Everything, it was all just too much, and a person could only handle a certain amount before breaking. Before giving up.

She crawled to the rear of the shed, as close to the heating vent as she could, and curled up in a fetal position.

More cops would come. Once they realized the helicopter pilot never responded to their requests for updates...

Yes.

They would come. They would find the Bigfoot in the cabin and the monster outside the shed. They would find poor Brett.

Would they check inside the shed too? Would they find her in the back curled up and asleep?

Or would they focus on the bodies and not realize she might be dying alone in the shed?

Questions without answers.

And...wasn't that the most frightening? Not knowing anything and unable to change or stop it?

Eventually exhaustion crept in and she drifted away on the gray waves of sleep where only her dreams would keep her company.

And the gnashing of bloodstained teeth...

THE END

Check out other great

Cryptid Novels!

Ian Faulkner

CRYPTID

Be careful what you look for. You might just find it.1996. A group of 14 students walked into the trackless virgin forests of Graham Island, British Columbia for a three-day hike. They were never seen again. 2019. An American TV crew retrace those students' steps to attempt to solve a 23-year-old mystery.A disparate collection of characters arrives on the island. But all is not as it seems. Two of them carry dark secrets. Terrible knowledge that will mean death for some – but a fighting chance of survival for others. In the hidden depths of the forests – man is on the menu. Some mysteries should remain unsolved...

Eric S. Brown

LOCH NESS HORROR

The Order of the Eternal Light, a secret organization have foretold the end of the human race. In order to save all humanity, agents of the Order must locate the Loch Ness Monster and obtain a sample of its blood for within in it is the key to stopping the apocalypse but finding the monster will be no easy task.

Check out other great

Cryptid Novels!

Hunter Shea

THE DOVER DEMON

The Dover Demon is real...and it has returned. In 1977, Sam Brogna and his friends came upon a terrifying, alien creature on a deserted country road. What they witnessed was so bizarre, so chilling, they swore their silence. But their lives were changed forever. Decades later, the town of Dover has been hit by a massive blizzard. Sam's son, Nicky, is drawn to search for the infamous cryptid, only to disappear into the bowels of a secret underground lair. The Dover Demon is far deadlier than anyone could have believed. And there are many of them. Can Sam and his reunited friends rescue Nicky and battle a race of creatures so powerful, so sinister, that history itself has been shaped by their secretive presence? "THE DOVER DEMON is Shea's most delightful and insidiously terrifying monster yet." – Shotgun Logic Reviews "An excellent horror novel and a strong standout in the UFO and cryptid subgenres." –Hellnotes "Non-stop action awaits those brave enough to dive into the small town of Dover, and if you're lucky, you won't see the Demon himself!" – The Scary Reviews PRAISE FOR SWAMP MONSTER MASSACRE "B-horror movie fans rejoice, Hunter Shea is here to bring you the ultimate tale of terror!" – Horror Novel Reviews "A nonstop thrill ride! I couldn't put this book down." – Cedar Hollow Horror Reviews

Armand Rosamilia

THE BEAST

The end of summer, 1986. With only a few days left until the new school year, twins Jeremy and Jack Schaffer are on very different paths. Jeremy is the geek, playing Dungeons & Dragons with friends Kathleen and Randy, while Jack is the jock, getting into trouble with his buddies. And then everything changes when neighbor Mister Higgins is killed by a wild animal in his yard. Was it a bear? There's something big lurking in the woods behind their New Jersey home.Will the police be able to solve the murder before more Middletown residents are ripped apart?

Check out other great

Cryptid Novels!

P.K. Hawkins

THE CRYPTID FILES

Fresh out of the academy with top marks, Agent Bradley Tennyson is expecting to have the pick of cases and investigations throughout the country. So he's shocked when instead he is assigned as the new partner to "The Crag," an agent well past his prime. He thinks the assignment is a punishment. It's anything but.Agent George Crag has been doing this job for far longer than most, and he knows what skeletons his bosses have in the closet and where the bodies are buried. He has pretty much free reign to pick his cases, and he knows exactly which one he wants to use to break in his new young partner: the disappearance and murder of a couple of college kids in a remote mountain town.Tennyson doesn't realize it, but Crag is about to introduce him to a world he never believed existed: The Cryptid Files, a world of strange monsters roaming in the night. Because these murders have been going on for a long time, and evidence is mounting that the murderer may just in fact be the legendary Bigfoot.

Gerry Griffiths

DOWN FROM BEAST MOUNTAIN

A beast with a grudge has come down from the mountain to terrorize the townsfolk of Porterville. The once sleepy town is suddenly wide awake. Sheriff Abel McGuire and game warden Grant Tanner frantically investigate one brutal slaying after another as they follow the blood trail they hope will eventually lead to the monstrous killer. But they better hurry and stop the carnage before the census taker has to come out and change the population sign on the edge of town to ZERO.

Made in the USA
Monee, IL
09 June 2022

97771083R00075